Praise for G

"What a beautiful introduction to m............ity for caregivers and children to cultivate together!"

—Dr. Christopher Willard, faculty at
Harvard Medical School and author of *Alphabreaths*

"Among the many wonderful mindfulness books for children, *Grow with Me Poetry* is a rare gem! Whimsical poems employ humor and rhyme to encourage children to develop self-awareness, understand their feelings, and appreciate the beauty in the world around them. Thoughtful questions and activities and enticements for journaling and drawing will help both novice and expert introduce mindfulness to children as a way of life. As someone who grew up reading and writing poetry as a part of family activities, I personally loved Fowler's focus on facilitating the relationship and connection between older and younger generations through poetry. This unique collection will be treasured by parents, caregivers, teachers, therapists, and all the children in their lives."

—Vivian Sisskin, Clinical Professor,
Dept. of Hearing and Speech Sciences, University of Maryland

"*Grow with Me Poetry* is an ingenious pairing of the lilting rhythm of rhyme with the practice of mindfulness. Research has evidenced the far-reaching impact of mindfulness for social and emotional wellbeing. When well taught and regularly practiced, mindfulness has been shown to help improve mood, self-esteem, self-regulation, and behavior. What better way to teach mindfulness than through the art of poetry! The poems generate curiosity, while encouraging open mindedness, gratitude, and appreciation. Learning and practicing mindfulness throughout the book serves to enhance the appreciation of poetry, and the developing love of the poems will encourage the mastering of mindfulness. A 'win-win' for sure."

—Kathleen V. O'Keefe, licensed clinical
social worker and private practitioner specializing in the
behavioral healthcare of children and adolescents

"As we face unprecedented incidences of stress, anxiety, and depression among our children, *Grow with Me Poetry* provides parents and educators alike with a timely and gentle response. What a special gift! With her creative and unique combination of mindfulness and poetry, Bridgette Fowler's *Grow with Me Poetry* offers an easy-to-use, heartwarming, and fun way to move beyond the sense of separation increasingly experienced by today's young people."

—Richard TenEyck, former superintendent,
former Assistant Commissioner of Education (NJ)

GROW WITH ME POETRY

by Bridgette Fowler

BELLE ISLE BOOKS
www.belleislebooks.com

Copyright © 2020 by Bridgette Fowler

No part of this book may be reproduced in any form or by any electronic or mechanical means, or the facilitation thereof, including information storage and retrieval systems, without permission in writing from the publisher, except in the case of brief quotations published in articles and reviews. Any educational institution wishing to photocopy part or all of the work for classroom use, or individual researchers who would like to obtain permission to reprint the work for educational purposes, should contact the publisher.

ISBN: 978-1-951565-24-4

LCCN: 2019919976

Cover and interior designed by Michael Hardison
Project managed by Haley Simpkiss

cover image: Adobe stock photo #141168922 (Family holding young sprout in hands by Sunny Studio).

Printed in the United States of America

Published by
Belle Isle Books (an imprint of Brandylane Publishers, Inc.)
5 S. 1st Street
Richmond, Virginia 23219

BELLE ISLE BOOKS
www.belleislebooks.com

belleislebooks.com | brandylanepublishers.com

I dedicate this book to my muse, and to all of the people and situations serendipitously placed along my poetic path; the listeners, the cheerleaders, those who found themselves entwined within the lines of my poems, my editor who ever so gently cultivated my writing prowess, and of course, to my publisher, who allowed my vision to be printed, bound, and ready for its new home on your bookshelf. To one and all, I thank you.

Introduction

I recently parted with a tired, worn-out old bookcase. It didn't always have the "vintage" look it has now. In its heyday, it was a booklover's dream: solid wood, with a rich walnut stain and two shelves that could proudly hold the weight of Google's illustrious predecessor: a complete set of encyclopedias. Its first home was a cozy hallway between two bedrooms and across from the bathroom in my grandmother's house. I remember how the sun from the bathroom window would illuminate the lace doily that sat on its top. When you pulled the perfect book from its shelf, a light thud would follow, as the bookcase teetered on the equally worn carpet and thumped against the wall.

My grandmother was an avid reader. She read anything and everything—newspapers, rag magazines, and harlequin romance novels; then Stephen King novels for a suspenseful twist. Every time I visited, I would make a beeline for that bookcase. A cup of tea and lively discussion with my grandmother would follow each finished book. It was the first and best book club I ever belonged to.

When I grew up, that sturdy little bookcase made its way into my home, and twenty-three years later, it was loaded into a trailer and moved to my daughter's first apartment, where it now holds the books that will set her on her life's path.

Along with that bookcase, the love of reading has been passed down through the generations. I wasn't very outgoing as a child; I preferred the drama in fiction to the real-life drama of childhood. Reading nourished my spirit as much as a gaggle of friends ever could. As I grew, like my grandmother, I continued to read, and read. My twin sister and I would walk a mile each way to check out books from the local library. (I can still remember the smell of that library—a lofty mix of dust, leather, and ink that only a true book buff could appreciate.) Our parents were teachers, and their yearly teachers' convention always yielded a new Trixie Beldon, Hardy Boys, or Nancy Drew book for our home. Eventually, that collection of books was compiled into a new library of sorts—housed in my grandmother's trusty old bookcase, which by then had relocated to my parents' house.

Over the years, my childhood reads gave way to textbooks and the research articles that would eventually launch my career. Time raged by, and suddenly I was married and reading to my own two toddlers. I needed to pass on the reading torch—but the task was more daunting than I had expected.

As in many households, bedtime was story time, though in our house it routinely ended with a child shouting, "Wake up, Mama, the BOOK IS NOT DOOONE!" How did other people work this nightmare of a routine? It seemed that while other parents were able to manage cooking, cleaning, parenting, working, and putting their children to bed while lovingly reading them a bedtime story, I found myself ill-equipped to handle all these tasks. My children helped me make my morning coffee. We cooked simple meals together. My house was clean, but not tidy—laundry had a way of piling up. And I routinely fell asleep before their bedtime story was finished.

This inability to "keep up" was the genesis for my poetry. It was my lifeline to a new bedtime routine, and the driving force behind the creation of what our family now refers to as "Nite-Notes." They came in the form of a scrapbook given to each of my children, which I left on their pillows at night—an improvised solution that allowed my children to practice reading while putting themselves to bed. It was a win-win! My Nite-Notes came in the form of poetry, jokes, and drawings that were specific to each child's day, frustrations, behaviors, and accomplishments. The first poem inside went something like this:

> *Roses are red,*
> *it is now time for bed,*
> *Mommy loves you*
> *and Daddy does too!*

More years flew by, I honed my rhyming skills, my children's independence soared, and their Nite-Notes eventually found a home on the bookshelf, nestled in among their other childhood favorites. To this day, I gift family members with a poem to mark all their special occasions.

Just like the books in my grandmother's bookcase, my Nite-Notes prompted ongoing family discussions. I found my children were talking to me and to each other about what I had written for them the night before. My poems actually facilitated conversations other than, "How was your day?" "Fine." Most importantly and unexpectedly, these conversations became my most treasured family time.

I wish I could have said, Voilà, done; problem solved!—but this was not the case. The life of any parent is hectic, but I found mine particularly unwound due to an undiagnosed genetic disorder that I now understand had been lurking in the background all those years, barging into my days repeatedly without invitation. It left me physically and mentally drained. The Nite-Notes had gifted me a new bedtime routine that afforded me more time to rest before going to bed; but I found I needed peaceful rest. As my head hit the pillow each night, my mind churned with the stress of maintaining some sense of normalcy despite my chronic medical concerns. Mindfulness was a practice that I welcomed into my life, in my efforts to find that quiet place before sleep. In doing so, I learned that mindfulness is a way of life.

Grow with Me Poetry allows me to share what I found to be the most rewarding aspects of Nite-Notes: poetry, mindfulness, and "bookcase" memories. You can think of each poem in Grow with Me Poetry as my Nite-Notes to you and your family.

To fully embrace your Nite-Notes, you must first gift yourself some quiet reading time. Poetry is well suited for a fast-paced lifestyle: although it's best read at leisure, little leisure time is required to read one poem. Embrace each poem in its duality: as a mindfulness practice entwined with poignancy. In becoming familiar with the practice and the poems, you will be better equipped to pass on what you have learned to your children.

In recalling that mindfulness calls us to place our attention on the present, reading the poetry aloud should be an important component of your practice. Your ability to be "in the moment" is heightened as you become aware of your intonation, your volume, the flow and speed of your reading, and the chime of the rhymes as you hear the written words in your own voice. In the initial pages of Grow with Me Poetry, you will be reading to pre-readers, but as your journey moves to the early readers, read to them first, and then encourage them to read aloud back to you! If you or your child are unaccustomed to reading poetry out loud, it can help to think of each poem as a song or schoolyard chant. The words in each line have natural stresses and breaks. Practice reading the poems out loud prior to reading them to your children, and if you need to, clap along until you get the rhythm. It might take you a couple tries, but the rhyme will come in time. Then, after you read to your children, talk to them; inspire them; and when they are ready, encourage them to read for themselves.

While they remain decidedly G-rated, as the poems progress you will find their content matures, acting as a window into your child's inner life and reflecting some of what they may be feeling as they develop. This is your opportunity to open that window and start a dialogue about whatever topics have been covered by the night's poems. Watch your child grow as the pages turn. When your child has become adept at reading on their own, and you feel the content in the later poems is age-appropriate, it will be time to pass the book to them. A reminder to do so will be found in the Postscripts. You will see Activities for You and Your Growing Child change into Activities for You (and

Your Parents Too). At this point, the activities are theirs exclusively. However, there will be instances where your child will be asked to seek out an adult to initiate a discussion. Be ready! Arm yourself by pre-reading the rest of the poems before handing the book over, and familiarize yourself with the questions they will be prompted to ask. During this transitional period, it may also be helpful to introduce the established reader to Grow with Me Poetry's first few pages. Even though you will have seeded and facilitated the practice of mindfulness, the initial chapters are a good reference for a sprouting child. Rest assured, while your child will come to hold the book, you will have held onto the content. In a world where we keep our children exceedingly busy, we often forget two important things: how to live in the present, and how to communicate with those we love the most. My hope is that these poems will serve as a catalyst for both.

Seed, sprout, and bloom illustration stamps have been included above each poem to serve as a quick reference guide to which age group the poem may best suit. Generally speaking, "seeds" are planted for late preschool and elementary school ages, "sprouts" grow into late elementary and middle school, and "blooms" flower into later middle school and mid-high school ages. Of course, parents are free to take liberties in matching their child's maturity to a poem's content, depending on the individual child's emotional development. "Postscripts" have also been included to assist you as you read. After each poem, you will find a "P.S." and a "P.S.S.," described below.

P.S. Here lies an afterthought, your **Poetry Simplified.** It serves as a glimpse into either the reason the poem was written, or an explanation of the poem itself. You may be surprised to learn that sometimes, the actual thought that precipitates a poem can be very trivial, even if the meaning behind it is not.

P.S.S. Here lies your space to facilitate communication with your children and family—your **Personal Soul Space**. If you are reading to or with your children, you will be prompted to journal here. At first you will be journaling for your children, letting them dictate their thoughts and feelings for you to record. If you have grown into this book and are journaling for yourself, you are the keeper of your pen, pencil, or crayon! The blank scroll after each journal page is for drawing what the poem elicits, either prompted or spontaneous.

I often look back to my own children's Nite-Notes with fond memories—though only when I am able to steal their books away from them, as they are now fully grown and keep them in their memory boxes. My hope is that you will bring your family together to read, engage, and laugh over the poems in this book, and in doing so, be as inspired to share them with others as I was to share them with you.

A Word on Mindfulness

I came to this practice fairly late in my life, by which time my kids were already grown up and at the helms of their own mental well-being. But I have found it beneficial in so many ways, I can't help but wonder how many times I may have been able to ease, if not totally alleviate, life's stresses had I simply started practicing mindfulness earlier. At the very least, I may have been able to better appreciate the sweet amid the sour.

The peace I feel in practicing mindfulness makes me wish I'd had the opportunity to teach my children how to incorporate mindfulness into their lives at a younger age. Mindfulness acts almost as preventative medicine, bolstering the soul against hardships and protecting the spirit as they occur. My Nite-Notes were a wonderful tradition for our family, and earned me a gold star in momsmanship. But as I embraced mindfulness more and more, I began to wonder if the format could be used to teach more than just reading skills. What if, through poetry, the practice of mindfulness could be introduced to young minds long before they ever need it? Through that notion came A Mindful Rhyme in Time.

What Is Mindfulness?

I define mindfulness as the practice of being acutely aware of what you are doing or feeling at any given moment. When you are being mindful, you are not meant to push away any thoughts, emotions, or sensations that you experience. Instead, you are encouraged to simply be aware of what you are experiencing, without assigning meaning or value to what creeps in. In its essence, mindfulness is pure observation, without judgement.

In defining what mindfulness is, it is often also helpful to define what it is not. Here are some common myths about mindfulness.

Myth #1: Mindfulness is religion-based. While it is most

known to be rooted in Buddhist philosophy, mindfulness is not exclusive to any one faith. It can be practiced by anyone, and is suited for everyone. It is, however, tied to the Buddhist philosophy that one should never intentionally impose harm upon another. It is a caring attention to the present moment, the practice of which does not endorse any particular religion or belief system. It would be an oxymoron to announce that you were mindful whilst pontificating from a bully pulpit. That is not caring attention to the present moment—not the mindful way.

Myth #2: Mindfulness can only be practiced during meditation. In my early practice of mindfulness, I was guilty of this belief. I thought that my meditation time was my mindful time. However, mindfulness can be practiced anytime, anywhere, and I find that it is best incorporated into one's daily routine.

Myth #3: Mindfulness will fix you. There is probably no better way to perpetuate a problem than to avoid the professionals trained to address the heart of the problem itself. Mindfulness is a tool always worth keeping in your emotional toolbox, but it is no substitute for appropriate medical care when medical care is necessary. I implore you to seek out proper medical attention should you have any concern for yourself or your child's medical or behavioral well-being.

Myth #4: Mindfulness must be practiced in solitude. I am glad this is not true; otherwise, this book would surely be a bust! If we can first learn for ourselves what it means to be mindful, then we can bequeath the practice to our children. When we are engaged in an activity with our children, being present in the moment serves to bring us together. Everyone using their cell phones or playing their own games with the TV blaring in the background promotes an air of separation and isolation. Parent and child practicing a simple breathing exercise, reading a poem in a mindful way, and then engaging in an activity promotes unity—the unity that comes from each participant being mindfully aware of the other, themselves, and the activity.

Myth #5: The goal of mindfulness is to "empty your mind." Quite the contrary! Mindfulness requests only the polite dignity of recognition. If you are taking a mindful walk outside, you are engaging all of your senses, making yourself aware of what you smell, the breeze you might feel, or simply the ground beneath your feet. If your thoughts begin to churn, simply let yourself be aware of them, much in the way you are aware of a child's relentless chatter when you are knee-deep in the middle of something and their tiny mouths cannot rest. Mindfulness is a clever tool you can use to keep thoughts moving through your mind in a beneficial way.

Lastly, a word on judgment. Mindfulness stresses the need to be kind to yourself as you learn your new skill. Should you experience unwanted thoughts, or if you find yourself paralyzed by what you think or feel, mindfulness gently asks you to acknowledge your thoughts, remove your self-judgement, and begin again. Self-judgement is self-destructive, and as you increase your ability to be mindful, inversely, your self-judging nature will decrease.

Why Practice Mindfulness?

Among the many benefits of practicing mindfulness, I find these most striking:

#1: Mindfulness can reduce anxiety. When we are focusing on what is, we are less likely to ruminate on what was or what might be. Thoughts involving the past and the future are what fuel anxiety. If we can stop perseverating on those thoughts, we can reduce anxiety.

For example, I happen to hate spiders. When I was about fifteen, I opened my closet one morning while getting ready for school, only to find an arachnid the size of my hand crouching about a foot away from my nose. My mother came running at the sound of my shriek, and, speechless, I could only gasp and point at the ghastly monstrosity. It was easily "re-homed" to the vacuum's canister, but the experience scarred me for life.

Nowadays, I live in the midst of a spiders' haven, on a beautiful fourteen-acre wooded lot. Since they occasionally decide to wander inside my house, if I allowed myself to think any further than I hate spiders when I saw one, I might be forced to up and move away from my lovely home. I need to hear myself say "Ick, a spider," and then let that thought go.

An emotional response is mediated by certain areas that are stimulated in the brain. Multiple studies over the past two decades have discussed this very mechanism, and validated that there is indeed an area of the brain that is linked to mindfulness and anxiety reduction.

I write in jest about my fear of spiders. How nice would that be if that were the only fear I needed to manage? But children's fears bloom so early, and as our world churns, so too do the bellies of our youth. To arm them with this simple but valuable life skill is a lasting gift.

#2: Mindfulness can increase attention. Recent studies have shown that practicing mindfulness can significantly improve working memory, visuospatial processing, and executive functioning. In today's society, technology and distraction call out to our children in an unprecedented way, and we are coming to understand how the daily use of technology (cell phones, computers, etc.) has more impact on young, developing brains than we ever imagined. We need tools that speak to our children's daily needs; tools that are not cumbersome and that don't burden us financially. How handy that mindfulness, as such a tool, might also combat the emerging darker side of technology's incessant call.

#3: Finally, as adults, we give our children so many things to attend to, and then their brains add to that list exponentially to the point of becoming distracted. We need only to think back one generation to see differences in the amounts of academic homework, involvement in organized sports, and employment that children are fitting into their lives. Our children's schedules have become frenzied. We, and they, can be their own worst enemies. Mindfulness offers an enticing option to remediate this troublesome issue.

How Can a Mindfulness Practice Be Applied to Poetry?

When I was first learning what it meant to be mindful, I found it most helpful to engage in visualization exercises. They gave me a greater understanding of what it meant to "be in the moment," and to practice a conscious awareness of the role our senses play in the process. What follows is an exercise that depicts mindfulness as it is entwined within the reading of a poem. Read through the exercise and then close your book and begin again by randomly selecting any poem within Grow with Me Poetry. Read the poem using all of the mindful prompts listed below. Once finished, you will have mindfully read your first poem!

Sit comfortably and take a nice deep breath in through your nose and then let it back out slowly through your mouth. Focus on the book in your hands. As you do:

1. Hear the slight cracking noise the binding makes as you open the book (the sense of hearing).
2. Notice the light aroma of the pages (the sense of smell).
3. Feel and hear the book's pages fan beneath your fingers as you pick out a poem (the tactile and hearing senses).
4. Feel the texture of the page as your finger sweeps across it (the tactile sense).
5. Notice the contrast of the ink with the page color (the visual sense).
6. Notice where the punctuation falls within the lines of the poem and how that affects your intonation as you

read (the visual and hearing senses).
7. Notice the rhythm of the poem (the hearing sense).
8. Pick out the rhymes in the poem (the visual and hearing senses).
9. Notice the volume and quality of your voice as you read the poem out loud (the hearing sense).

You may find that as you read certain poems, varying thoughts or emotions creep into your experience. For example:

1. That poem really reminded me of someone!
2. Hmm, they haven't called me in a long time.
3. I wonder if I have done something to upset them.
4. Should I call them or let them call me?
5. I can feel my nerves like butterflies in my belly!

This leads to one of the most important aspects of a mindfulness experience and practice:

1. Bring your thoughts back to the sensations surrounding the poem itself.
2. Let the anxiety-provoking thoughts come and go. You will find that as you focus on the poem, they will!
3. If you are feeling nervous, acknowledge the "butterfly" sensation in your stomach before guiding your thoughts back to the poem itself.
4. Allow yourself to be present in the moment as you are enjoying reading your poem. You are not living in the past or future, but in "the now."

Even as you move through different thoughts and emotions while in the moment, you have moved yourself back to the act itself with conviction, and you are taking care not to be critical as or if you happen to stray—the mindful way.

Mindfulness is innate to children. It is why they might not immediately respond when you call out to them. They are totally (mindfully) engrossed in the task at hand and your voice becomes the background chatter! You can use this to your advantage and simply role model what you have learned, then revel while they absorb your actions and behaviors as they apply to different situations, in this case, poetry. When reading poetry to children, should they become distracted, gently redirect them by prompting them to listen to the sound of your voice as you read to them. Older children will be able to appreciate the exercise above for themselves. With practice, your child will be able to stay "in the moment" for longer periods of time. Dually, you have also assured your child that there is no need to place judgment or value on something that needn't be judged or valued at that particular time. Remember to tell your child what you heard, felt, or thought about. It may help them put their own thoughts into words.

How Can I Promote the Successful Practice of Mindfulness?

Since mindfulness asks you not to focus on distractions, eliminate as many as you can prior to your mindful reading time. First, dress for success! If you or your child are uncomfortable, you will not want to sit for five minutes to practice or read, even if you like what you are reading. Second, set up your own "mindful time" spot, one that is conducive to quiet fun and set away from distractions. Make sure that your spot is not also where your child completes homework, as that location may have a negative emotional association. Lastly, make sure to have your journaling and drawing materials all ready to go!

Now Let's Start!

The following three poems serve as a guide—practice poems, if you will. It's important to remember that you do not have to be an expert in mindfulness to begin reading to your children. The joy is that you are learning and growing together.

A Clue

Join me in reading these poems today
And we'll learn how to read in the mindful way
What does that mean? Speak the words in your head
The answer will lie in the words you have read
First look at the letters, how they form a thin line
Hear the bounce of the words and the way that they rhyme
If thoughts or distractions should holler and shout
Like clouds in the sky, let them float in, through, and out
Now try this: place your finger where the pages all meet
Feel it sandwiched in the middle of the left and right sheets
To glide it up and then over is the mission at hand
In search of those ridges where your fingers should land
Let the pages fan down from the front to the back
As you select the next one, now you're getting the knack!
Did you hear the light crinkle as you gave it a turn?
It might take a few tries, but with practice you'll learn
Now imagine each word written solely for you
Every poem a guide that will offer a clue
To that treasure of stillness, that soft quiet place
Where you and your soul may share an embrace.

P.S. Consider this poem an introduction to mindfulness. I found the practice most daunting at first, and I wondered how it could be introduced in a fun and simple way. My hope is that by reading this short poem, you might understand the practice a little better. Read each poem as directed by "A Clue." Use it as a refresher, should you begin to forget your "mindful" way.

P.S.S. Questions and Activities for You and Your Growing Child

1. *What do you perceive are the benefits of mindfulness?*
2. *How might you describe mindfulness to your children?*

___

___

___

___

___

___

___

___

___

___

___

___

___

Breathe

Take a deep breath right up through your nose
Inhale as if smelling a lovely red rose
The sensation is cool as you breathe up and in
Now hold it one—two, then back out again.
Breathe into your nose, and then out through your mouth
Notice your shoulders as they find their way south
If stray thoughts keep creeping into your mind
Try counting your breaths and you'll leave them behind
Practice your new skill at least once a day
Before reading a poem might be the best way
You'll soon find your happy place deep down within
So breathe back in slowly, then back out again.

P.S. Prana Yama, the breath of life, is what sustains and calms us. Did you know that you are physically unable to "panic" while engaged in a breathing exercise? We are adept at multitasking, yet the brain is physically incapable of engaging in "fight or flight" while we are consciously attending to our breath. This is why it is so powerful, and why it is essential to focus on your breath in times of stress.

A breathing exercise is also a simple means of introducing the relaxation practices that are so essential to mindfulness. That simple action can bring us to a state of being able to clear our thoughts, empty our minds, and ready ourselves for the day. "Breathe" is a starting place! Make sure to squeeze in at least two or three deep breaths before beginning to read a poem.

P.S.S. Questions and Activities for You and Your Growing Child

1. How can you incorporate breathing exercises into your day?

2. When would it be helpful to encourage your child to stop and do a breathing exercise?

3. At what times of the day or in what situations do you think a breathing exercise might be in order?

Monkey Mind

The constant chatter
A continuing clatter
A muddled confusion
A distant illusion
The revolving door
Of distractions galore
Never stopping to rest
Each vying to test
Our patience worn thin
From places we've been
In one single second
Our minds can't reckon.
Best to breathe deeply and try to sit still
In order to tame your monkey mind's will.

P.S. I just love this phrase, "monkey mind!" It's such a fun visual: one monkey starts chattering away, and then another joins in, and soon your whole mind is screeching like a zoo!

A child's monkey mind might sound like this: "I raised my hand in school, the teacher didn't call on me, she never calls on me; she doesn't like me; no one likes me; I have no friends—" and so on. Every thought is another monkey screeching.

In this poem, I wanted to build on this idea to explore how stray thoughts can add to the frenzy of our lives, reminding us when we get overwhelmed to just go back and refocus on our breath.

P.S.S. Questions and Activities for You and Your Growing Child

1. How are you honing your mindfulness skill?

2. If you find you are constantly hounded by your thoughts, try writing them down below, and then read through the poem again. If they persist, try this little exercise:

Let's pretend that you and your child are walking around a zoo. At the moment, you would like to pay attention to an adorable baby elephant who is reaching its trunk out to you. High above, there are monkeys swinging on vines. You see them, but don't need to pay them any mind; they are simply there.

All of those monkeys are your thoughts. You see them swooping all around, and every once and a while, a pesky one demands that you pay attention to it by screeching as loud as it can. When that happens, try to watch that one monkey grab onto another vine and swing away. If he swoops in again, acknowledge him, give him a banana, and watch him saunter off smiling.

This little exercise shows your child how to acknowledge their thoughts without reacting to them (by being aware of the monkeys swinging on vines overhead), and then allows them to take control of moving the thoughts through their mind (by visualizing the monkey swinging on out, or being acknowledged—by being given a banana—before moving along). If the exercise doesn't work, it is time to go back to your breathing exercises to stop that "monkey business" for good!

Grow with Me Poetry – A Mindful Rhyme in Time

Can you find the lesson that like a gem shines?

   The pearls of wisdom between the lines

      Focus on your breath if overcome by the clatter

         To stay in the moment, despite your mind's chatter

            Now lying ahead are the rhymes I bestow

               Keep turning the pages, and with them, you'll gr0W…

What Am I?

I was born to you on day one.
I think I was made just for fun,
Halfway between your head and your toes,
Smack in between your feet and your nose,
Serving no purpose but to catch some lint—
Now that right there is the hint of all hints!
If you poke me right here, I might just giggle!
If not, then surely, with your belly I'll wiggle.
I'm big enough to house a single green pea,
But if I'm an "outtie," then I won't fit a flea.
Should Mr. Pointer find his way there,
"Home sweet home!" with a grin he'd declare.
Now is the time to guess; do you know?
Your tummy holds the answer; just look below.
Tuck your head down to see your middle.
If you yelled, "MY BELLY BUTTON,"
    you solved the riddle!

P.S. I wrote this poem for adults and children alike, as a wonderful little exercise in mindfulness. In reading it, you can't help but become aware of the content and nothing else. This poem allows you to focus on the words, the pictures they create, and their overall silliness.

If you experienced distractions while reading, try reading this poem one more time. Allow the distractions to float right over the page from one side to the next, just as your eyes follow the words from left to right. Allow yourself to know that they are there, but pay them no mind. Read the poem until the end. You have just experienced seventeen lines of mindfulness.

P.S.S. Questions and Activities for You and Your Growing Child

1. As an adult, were you able to give the words your full attention? If not, know that you are not the judge and jury; you are a student. You are learning. Keep reading, and your skill will progress!

2. As you read this poem to your child, let it be an interactive experience. "What Am I?" is a poem that encourages a "tickle," a poem that begs you to use your "outdoor voice" when prompted by BIG PRINT—and it is a poem where Mr. Pointer, your index finger, must act out his part. In doing so, notice your child is focused solely upon you and your actions. Children come by mindfulness honestly. Learn from their little beings and enjoy the moments you can share in a mindful way.

3. Record your experience as you read this poem to your child.

4. Help your child to draw themselves, complete with a big belly button!

Good Night Words

Stupid is one of the worstest of words
Out of your mouth it should never be heard
Why, you might ask, is that word SO bad?
Because, I will tell you, it makes people sad
A much better word would be the word smart
Now that is a fantabulous place to start!
Why, you persist, should it start with me?
Because, I reply, smart is what I'd like to be
Hate is a word even worse than the worst
To shout it, of course, is a hurtful outburst
Love is a magical word when it's spoken
Because when it's said, then your heart can't be broken
"You're smart—you are smart," I say it again
"I love you, I love you." Sleep tight now,

THE END.

P.S. I wrote this while thinking about what makes children feel good and what makes children feel bad. Sympathy and empathy are not always innate, and I believe children need to feel special in order to be special. I hope you will read this poem with your child over and over. Teach them what thoughts make us feel good, and what thoughts make us feel bad. Make them feel smart; make them feel loved. The written word turns into the spoken word—poetry in motion.

P.S.S. Questions and Activities for You and Your Growing Child

1. Have your child tell you two words that make them feel good. Ask them why.

2. Have your child tell you two words that make them feel sad. Ask them why.

3. Record their words. As you reread the poem and repeat this exercise, watch how the words they dictate change as they mature.

4. Have your child draw a smiley face with a "happy" word above it.

5. Have your child draw a sad face with a "sad" word below it.

Time for A Walk

It's time for a walk, it will be fun, you'll see!
Put up your fingers in the shape of a V
Now as you turn your hand upside down
You have two little legs to walk all around!
Wheeeeee! up your arm to your shoulder they go
Zigging and zagging as they pass your elbow
Down to your heart they circle around
Zooming up to your face, your sniffer they found!
Like on a snare drum, they *tap-tap-tap-tap*
Then they skip on back down for a rest in your lap
All tuckered out, they know what to do
They just need a friend, for this you need two
So wave to your other hand, make them both meet
 Now clap three times and put them to sleep!

P.S. My husband created this game for my children: they would use their fingers as if they were legs running around, and hilarity would ensue. This poem was inspired out of their fun. It's a silly way to engage your child in a simple activity that can lead to treasured memories.

P.S.S. Questions and Activities for You and Your Growing Child

1. What is a silly game you have made up with your children? It is A-OK if this becomes your game!

2. Have your child draw their running-man hand. It may help to have them trace their hand as it sits in the upside-down shape of a peace sign!

_____

_____

_____

_____

_____

_____

_____

_____

_____

_____

_____

_____

Monsters

There is a monster living under my bed
I know it is real, not just in my head
So I did a handstand and looked upside down
But to my surprise, it was not to be found.

There's a monster behind the closet door in my room
Do I dare peek inside where I know it will loom?
I muster the courage and fling the door wide
Finding no monster to be seen there inside.

There is a monster that lives in my head
Not in my closet or under my bed
So I blink, blink, blink, and I think it away
For only me, myself, and I can keep it at bay.

So I say, "Hey Monster, go now, STAY AWAY!"
And off now it goes, without fuss or delay
Because there was a human that lived in *its* head
And it was me that he feared as I slept in my bed.

Monster, oh Monster, who's more scared of whom
As we hide from each other in the gloom of my room?
Might it be neither? For when it appears
The monster itself becomes our own fears.

P.S. Have you ever wondered why monsters come in so many shapes and forms? I think it is because they symbolize fear itself. When that realization hits us squarely on the forehead, I believe we are better able to keep our monsters at bay.

P.S.S. Questions and Activities for You and Your Growing Child

1. What "monster" lies under your bed, in your closet, or in your head? Ask your child the same question.

2. Have your child draw a picture of what their monster looks like. If you are reading for yourself, draw a picture of your monster, your fear, or what the poem "shows" you!

Them's SHOUT'N' Words!

We all should go ZZZOOOOM
    when leaving a room
and yell out SWIIIIISSSSHHH
    when using a broom
When dinner's a winner,
    we should bellow YUUUMMMMY
If you have a big burp,
    don't forget EXCUSE MEEEEEE
And remember to say PLEEEEEAAASE
    if you want a bit more
Then call out HOORAAAY!
    as your friend walks through the door
Shout BOOOOO! when you sneak up on
    that very same buddy
Who is sure to scream AHHHHHH!
    all high-pitched and funny
Add hooo to that booo
    and now cry out BOOOHOOO
For sadly, there's no more SHOUT'N' words for you!

P.S. I wrote this poem as I remembered reading to my children in their early years. They loved any time they could join in and shout out a word. I wrote this poem to let your children do just that. If they didn't do so the first time, reread this poem to them and encourage them to SHOUT out them SHOUT'N' words!

P.S.S. Questions and Activities for You and Your Growing Child

1. These SHOUT'N' words were loud! What other things make LOUD sounds? Write down what your child dictates!

2. Help your child draw something that makes a LOUD sound.

_____

_____

_____

_____

_____

_____

_____

_____

_____

_____

_____

_____

_____

Help your child draw something that makes a LOUD sound.

Purr, Please

Two tigers growled, then started to roar
'Til they had to back off or else settle the score
For in due kitty time
They'll forgive a cat crime
And purr as they once did before.

P.S. Children remind me of tigers when they argue, full of great roars and growls. We try to teach our children to take a step back when they are angry, go to a corner, cool down, and learn to forgive and forget. But this can be hard for little minds in the heat of the moment—so to help, I wanted to come up with a fun visual for children to call upon when they're feeling primal! "Purr, Please" could even work as a family mantra when you start to see a roar building up!

P.S.S. Questions and Activities for You and Your Growing Child

1. Ask your children to describe any arguments they had today, then any arguments they might have had "a long time ago." (Remember, their concept of time is a bit different from ours!) Ask them to describe the arguments and whether they can remember the old one as well as the new one. Discuss how memories can fade away, even though we were very angry or hurt at the time of the fuss. If they are holding any grudges, it might be helpful to describe those as a rumbling growl—one which they can then allow to fade into a purr.

2. With your help or by themselves, have your child draw a tiger. Is the tiger roaring or purring, fighting or happy?

With your help or by themselves, have your child draw a tiger.

Is the tiger roaring or purring, fighting or happy?

I Want It Now

I just have to have it—you simply must know
I cannot live without what I *need* in tow
I beg and persist and then start to plead
Give it here, right now—before me with speed!
But a want should not be confused with a *need*
We can do without one, though the other we heed
Now what is the difference between the two?
You'll find wants are many, but true *need*s are quite few
What keeps your heart beating is a definite *need*
While a want only lasts a short while indeed
Go forth and think carefully as you proceed
Do you simply want, or do you have a deep *need*?

P.S. I was inspired to write this poem after hearing a child wail his way through the toy aisle after being denied his **want**. *It happens to the best of us, and parents and grandparents alike have all heard "I want it now!" As adults, we think these four words in our heads all the time, but hopefully have come to understand when it is okay to give in to a* **want** *and when to heed a* **need**.

P.S.S. Questions and Activities for You and Your Growing Child

1. Write down or draw some of the things you, and then your child, **wanted** *this week. Discuss whether each of their "things" was a* **want** *or a* **need***. Explain why. Then write a big "W" or "N" next to each one. If you are writing for your child, make sure to give them some good examples of what you* **wanted** *versus what you* **needed***, and add them into the mix!*

2. Draw one picture of a **want** *with a "W" above it, and one picture of a* **need** *with a "N" above it.*

Toe the Line

Ow! My mama toe! I yelp now in pain
I tried hard to dodge, but alas, 'twas in vain
For atop cotton clouds, looking up, not ahead
Root-beer floating and thinking of ice cream instead.
Chocolate, strawberry, vanilla—those flavors
Topped with hot fudge, all the tastes that I savor
Nuts and bananas with whipped cream, then cherries
Tippity-topped by a wee band of fairies.
To those pixies I beckoned: *Now swoop to the ground*
Where me and my sad aching toe can be found
Wings all abuzz, they set me back on my feet
Sing-songing these words as they made their retreat:
Keep your eyes straight ahead as you toe a straight line
To ensure that your piggies will all be just fine
Then skip, jump, or hop without losing a beat
To that daydreamed delight that you just have to eat!

P.S. We've all gotten distracted while walking and suffered the consequences. I wrote this poem after an especially nasty run-in with my living room coffee table, as a reminder that mindfulness can be practiced anywhere, at any time—even while walking!

Every parent has seen their children skipping along, paying no mind but for the thoughts in their heads, their little piggies—and noggins—in peril. These nerve-wracking experiences serve as a good reminder that it is never too early to teach children that mindfulness is not meant to be used solely within the confines of poetry—you can mindfully walk too! In reminding your child to be "aware" of their surroundings—in other words to "be in the moment"— you might just save them a whole lot of hurt!

P.S.S. Questions and Activities for You and Your Growing Child

1. Ask your child what happens when they forget to look where they are going.

2. Ask your child what they daydream about.

3. Have your child draw a picture of what they daydream about, or maybe even a big stubbed mama toe!

GROW WITH ME POETRY

To Rattle a Tattle

I think I should tattle, but when do I dare?
There might be a fuss, so should I really care?
But you simply must shout
To help your pals out
If there's danger and they need to BEWARE!

P.S. I wrote this poem when I was first learning to write limericks. They are short, sweet, and a super way to deliver a message to little ones who have tiny attention spans! I found tattling particularly hard to parent and wished I had written this little limerick much earlier in life!

We all know that tattling over every little thing is a bad habit. But sometimes, a little tattle can be a BIG help. You see, most times we can handle problems on our own; but other times, we can't. When that happens, it's like accidentally floating into the deep end of a pool without your water wings—scary! That's when we definitely need to call out to a lifeguard. Learning the difference is just part of growing up!

Before you run to get that lifeguard (or any other adult), ask yourself: is someone getting hurt? Might someone get hurt later? Is there still danger, even if I've said or done all I can do to help? If the answer to any of these questions is YES, then it's time to go find a grown-up. Remember, telling shouldn't be done because you didn't get your way, or just to get someone in trouble—it should be done to help keep people out of trouble!

Parents, in helping your children to learn the difference between a helpful tattle and the kind that can do more harm than good, try posing a little twist of the poem's ending to them. In the midst of a tattling dilemma, ask them, "Is there danger, and does someone need to BEWARE?" A little humor can go a long way in teaching important life skills.

P.S.S. Questions and Activities for You and Your Growing Child

1. Discuss tattling with your child. When is tattling important, and when should we keep our tattletales to ourselves? Talk about how tattling is like blowing a whistle, alerting someone to danger!

2. Help your child draw a picture of someone blowing a big whistle. (Stick figures are fine!)

Help your child draw a picture of someone blowing a big whistle.

(Stick figures are fine!)

Hee Hee Hee

Silly is as silly was, bouncing around as she
    always does
Underlying the daily grind, a smile her goal,
    simply because
Silly's plan is to break the ice
With a *tap tap tap*, she'll rap more than twice
Persistent and knowing the results lie ahead
And before *you* know it, a crack has now spread
What starts as a chuckle ends in the song
Of a deep belly laugh that fully belongs
To all of us willing to sing out of tune
Never being afraid to act like a loon.

P.S. I wrote this as a reminder for parents to be silly! The further we get from childhood, and the more deeply we are buried in responsibilities, the harder it is to find the "silly" within ourselves. I think that is why children find it so funny when we let our guard down and let our silliness soar!

When my son was in elementary school, I became "the coolest" mom by doing one thing: I blew not one, but four bubbles inside of a single, gigantic bazooka bubble. It was a field day, it was hot, and I was encircled by a bunch of sweaty second-grade boys. What was a gum-chewing mom to do, other than demonstrate her insane bubble-blowing skills?

One of the little boys in the crowd told his mom about my great feat. Later, she relayed his shock and awe that an adult could, and would do such things. (And a MOM, no less!) That was when I learned the value of silliness.

P.S.S. Questions and Activities for You and Your Growing Child

1. Tell your child the silliest thing you have done to make someone laugh. What random act of silliness has your child performed to make you laugh?

2. Why are we afraid to be silly? Ask your child what they think.

3. Who is sillier, Mom or Dad? What do they do that is silly?

4. Draw a picture of you or your child being silly. Are you hopping, making a silly face, dancing, or laughing?

Such a Hullabaloo

Like on a big trampoline, I jumped up and down
Scrunching my face into the worst frown I could frown
As my legs buckled, I dropped onto the floor
Rolled all around, and let out a big roar!
Sent to my room until I could behave
My anger spilled over like a huge ocean wave
Now a fish out of water, I flipped and I flopped
Three words stuck in my head as I shouted and hopped
Gimmie, gimmie, GIMMIE; I must, I MUST
No, no, NO! as I fussed and I fussed
I thought I would scream the whole night long
Piercing and loud, my own special song
But as my eyes closed without my permission
Like a wand had been waved by a silent magician
I awoke to myself—the one I *should* be
Instead of the previously furious me
But wait! There are three *other* words I can say
To admit what happened and not sweep it away
Four lowly syllables reserved for such times
When forgiveness is needed for all of those crimes
So now here it comes, what lies ahead:
"I am sorry," genuinely said.

P.S. This poem was written for both adults and children. Aren't we all guilty of losing control sometimes? Often, it is how you deal with the aftermath that is more important than the loss of control itself.

I wrote this remembering two things: my own daughter's youngest years, and how awful it feels to lose control. It took me too long to realize that children are often lost to their emotions.

P.S.S. Questions and Activities for You and Your Growing Child

1. When was the last time you or your child wanted to stomp?

2. Are you mean to those around you when you feel angry? Is your child?

3. How hard is it to apologize? Practice saying sorry "like you mean it." Don't be afraid of sounding silly—remember "Hee Hee Hee"?

4. Draw a picture of yourself when you feel mad.

5. Draw a picture of yourself hugging the person you said you were sorry to.

Today Is the Day

Today is the day I will slay my day!
No more worries, I'll just throw them away
Staying upbeat, not stressed to the max
Trying my best to sit and relax
No dwelling, no telling, no staring beware
No fretting, no brooding, even though I do care
I am the focus of my life thus far
I am the driver of my own little car
I'll try my best to stay in my lane
Hoping my efforts will not be in vain
So bring it on, again now I say
Today is the day I will slay my day!

P.S. Many thanks to Kyle Gray, author of Raise Your Vibrations, Light Warrior, *and many other inspirational books, for introducing me to the phrase "slay my day." Those three words set me down the path of creating what I like to call an "intentional affirmation" poem. It was written to affirm that we are in control of our own persons and specifically voices an intention to make it so. I consider "Today Is the Day" the ultimate "refrigerator poem."*

P.S.S. Questions and Activities for You and Your Growing Child

1. Shout this out with your children at the beginning of their day!

2. Draw a picture of yourself "slaying your day"!

Draw a picture of yourself "slaying your day"!

My XX

The day you were born, a new world unfurled
Two simple Xs made you my girl
With a twirling dress and two ponytails bouncing
And that stubborn "s" you had trouble pronouncing
As my sweet caterpillar grew beautiful wings
With strength and endurance, you continued to sing
As you take your place and speak up in your world
I will always remember the way that you twirled
My punkin, my double-X, this you must know
Through your storm you emerged as a stunning rainbow.

For my little survivor,
XXOO,
Mama

P.S. This poem encapsulates my little girl. She was born in innocence and triumphed over personal adversity. This is my tribute to her.

P.S.S. Questions and Activities for You and Your Growing Child

1. Tell your child what you love about her. What was she like as a tyke? What has she triumphed over?

2. Now it is the reader's time to draw: create a picture of how you see your child. (Remember, stick figures with a happy face and a big heart will make your child's heart swell!)

_____

_____

_____

_____

_____

_____

_____

_____

_____

_____

_____

_____

_____

_____

_____

My XY

My first and my only, my quiet XY
Born unto me, and how lucky was I!
All full of cuddles, never shy with your love
You were truly a gift sent to me from above
Big brown eyes always yearning to see
The wonders before you and the man you'd be
Steadfast in your kindness, so honest and true
Such traits elusive to more than a few
Yet it comes so easily to my tall boy
You fill so many hearts with pride and with joy
A pillar of strength in times of great strife
Your calmness alone will lead you through life
As your dreams lie before you, it's just this I pray
That you know I will love you as I did yesterday.

For my Nate the Great,
All my love,
Madré

GROW WITH ME POETRY

P.S. You met my daughter above, so now, let me introduce my son. This poem was written for him. He is a quiet wonder who will never, ever understand the depths at which he touches the heart of every person he meets.

P.S.S. Questions and Activities for You and Your Growing Child

1. Tell your child the way they "touch the hearts" of others.

2. Draw a picture of a hand touching a heart!

Tickity-Tock

Knock-knock-knock, tickity-tock
I'm at your door as you watch the clock
Fine sand runs through the hourglass
A second, a minute, another will pass
Front and center, the Present does say
I'm here right now, do not wish me away!
Future waits patiently as Past says goodbye
Sure as the full moon hangs high in the sky
So keep Past and Future tucked safely away
With Present at hand, so you may cherish *each* day.

P.S. This was written as I was thinking of all the times I've wanted to warp-speed myself right through the present to come out sometime in the future. Since this is not yet possible, I thought of the many single moments making up the time I wanted to shirk. Even in those moments, I laughed; I appreciated a pink sky at night; I loved the sight of steam emanating from the hay bales I drove past every morning; and I have seen not one, but TWO double rainbows this year alone. To intentionally avoid adversity is to unintentionally miss splendor. To live in the past is to miss the present. You cannot have one without the other, any more than you can have peanut butter without jelly. (Well, you could, but that is just wrong!)

P.S.S. Questions and Activities for You and Your Growing Child

1. Help your child to understand that "past" means what was, the "present" is right now, and the "future" is what might happen next.

2. Ask your child if they are anticipating something. What is it?

3. Ask your child if there is something that happened to them recently that they can't stop thinking about.

4. Ask your child if these thoughts keep them from "seeing" what is around them every day. Ask them what they might notice or think about if they were not preoccupied with these thoughts. Remind them that if they look to see what can be seen, smell what can be smelled, and hear what can be heard, those thoughts may float away on their own—mindfulness in practice! Have them notice what they see, hear, or smell as you are talking together. Point out how they were unable to think of anything but what they were describing as they were doing so!

5. Draw a picture of what you remember seeing today. You may have to give yourself a little homework assignment to remember what you see each day, and then come back to this poem and draw!

Turf Time

Poking right up through the bare toes of your feet

Oh, how it tickles when first we meet!

Amidst the cold dew you might hastily race

But feeling my warmth will lessen your pace

On bright early mornings you might see me glisten

Blades of green glory, as you walk on me listen

Do I crinkle or snap when I fall under your foot?

Or gently indent at the earth where it's put?

Watch where you step, look down and then stare

Does a worker bee hide in my clover somewhere?

The depth of my carpet is a living delight

Nothing that lives here means to stir up a fright

So tiptoe, or race, or casually stroll

Tuck your chin down and somersault-roll!

My roots run deep, and here I will stay

A playground for all to be found where I lay.

 GROW WITH ME POETRY

P.S. I snuck a little exercise in mindfulness into this poem. How did you do?

Whether young or old, we all have a memory of grass. My hope is that as you read, you can feel the grass beneath your feet, tossing away all other thoughts and letting your mind do the walking.

P.S.S. Questions and Activities for You and Your Growing Child

1. When was the last time you played in the grass? Describe it! If you are reading with children, allow them to remember, feel, and describe how they played. Write down what they say, and read it back to them.

2. Draw a beautiful field of grass! Include the creatures that live there.

_____

_____

_____

_____

_____

_____

_____

_____

_____

_____

_____

A Wise Man Said...

A wise man's young daughter once sat at his knee
And told him *There's something that's troubling me.*
For try as she would, her voice felt trapped inside
As if from life's hard choices it wanted to hide
Her heart was weighed down and her mind full of chatter
With *Why this?* and *What if?* and *Does it all matter?*
And further perplexed, she heard two distinct voices
Which gave her conflicting and very hard choices
One voice was *tiny* and *so very small*
Yet it spoke of a truth that encompassed the All
But the other was **loud,** like a megaphone s h o u t i n g
Of the anger and worry that had left her heart doubting
She quietly spoke of the duel in her head
This tumbling out, the next words that she said

How can my tiny voice win out over the loud?
To her great surprise, her father was proud
Of the strength that it took to share
     what was so troubling
Then to ask for his help with what inside
     had been bubbling
So then from his wise lips in a casual drawl
He said, *You just feed the tiny 'til it grows tall*
But what should I feed it? she implored with a tear
Don't worry, he told her, *I'll make it quite clear*
Feed yourself time, and in time you will see
The voice that calls out will soon set you free
So she mustered the courage and did what he said
And her *tiny, meek* voice became **LOUD** in her head!
Time did pass by, and she often will say
What a wise man said to his daughter one day.

P.S. Daddies and daughters do talk. One day, my husband told me about a conversation he'd had with our daughter. It was so poignant that I felt called to write about it so our family would always remember that treasured conversation.

I find it fascinating that even children notice a difference between the voices representing what they should do versus what they want or feel pressured to do—whether that pressure be internal or external. I hope that this poem helps convey the words we all struggle to find as we teach our children how to listen to their own little voices.

If you look ahead, you will see that the P.S.S. sections from here on out have changed. They now read: Questions and Activities for You (and your Parent Too). Now is the time to consider if you would like put your children in charge of Grow with Me Poetry. *Assure your children that even though you are passing on the book, they are welcome to involve you in their experience at any time they would like, even outside future activities prompting them to do so. BUT, they do not have to. You have planted your seeds, now watch them spout and bloom!*

P.S.S. Questions and Activities for You (and Your Parents Too)

1. What is the wisest thing your father (or another influential person) has said to you? Conversely, ask your parents about their favorite things they have learned from you—the answers might surprise you!

2. What does your tiny voice whisper?

3. What does your **loud** *voice shout?*

4. Draw something that makes a loud sound, and then something that makes a quiet sound (for example, a lion and a mouse).

Draw something that makes a loud sound,

*and then something that makes a quiet sound
(for example, a lion and a mouse).*

I Need My Mom

One day I got sick and I needed my mother
There was no substitute, I wanted no other
How is one person so loving and dear
Silently comforting when they are near?
With motherly wisdom she innately sees
These moments in life come and go as they please
Now sitting before me, she has one request
In this moment we share, she just asks that I rest
As my eyes shut, then away she will creep
Only to appear as I wake from my sleep
Stroking my hair with a smile just for me
Shedding light onto who she has groomed me to be
Patient, persistent, hand stretched out to another
Are the lessons I've learned from the love of my mother.

P.S. I wrote this poem beside a hospital bed, after having comforted a young adult suffering through tremendous pain. Her mother had not been present in her life, and it made me think about the maternal presence with which I had been graced. I wrote this poem in honor of my mother and the kind of person she taught me to be.

P.S.S. Questions and Activities for You (and Your Parents Too)

1. When was the last time you wished your mother was with you? Remember that a mother can take many forms. If you do not have a mother, think instead of another very special and nurturing adult presence in your life.

2. What does your mother or mother figure do that makes you feel better when you're upset?

3. Sometimes our mothers or mother figures misunderstand our needs during times of distress! If you find this to be true, what is it that you need or want during these times? Share that need!

4. Draw a picture that represents "comfort." You might simply blend soothing colors together in a particular pattern, or draw something that makes you feel calm. Try it, and see what happens!

The Trip

With a *whoops* and a yell, I fell right on the ground!
As I lay there my peepers scanned all those around
Finding a million wide eyes staring down at me
Oh, to be invisible, for then they wouldn't see
Knowing I could no longer hide in plain sight
I jumped onto on my feet with all of my might
Proclaiming these words, as if speaking in jest:
It's okay, I'm fine, I just needed a rest!
Now a great tale, a memory stowed in its place
Triggered by seeing a flapping shoelace
So many trips and spectacular falls
And if I am lucky, the sound of applause
Will be the round started with my own two hands
Cheering myself for my silly grandstand.

GROW WITH ME POETRY

P.S. I wrote this poem wanting to explore one of the most important lessons of my life: how to use humor to carry me through awkward and embarrassing situations.

My husband, myself, and our two toddlers were the proud owners of our second home, and it was move-in day. The moving truck was backing into our steep driveway, and it was my job to gracefully direct its giant tires so they would avoid gouging the beautiful strip of green hilled lawn I was standing on. In doing so, I stepped in some random divot and proceeded to sausage-roll in several grand rotations right down to the bottom of the grassy knoll. As I lay there, splayed on my back, I looked toward our cul-de-sac and was mortified to see my new neighbors driving by, mouths gaping, having just met me from afar for the very first time. I waved and mouthed, "Hello!" It was the neighborly thing to do.

Out of my travels down our hill came "The Trip." Falls are inherently funny, but only if you allow yourself to see the humor through your embarrassment. In our family, it is common for a laugh to come before we ask, "ARE YOU OKAY?" Mind you, we most certainly care and tend to each other—but we appreciate the comedy of a grand slip, trip, or fall, and through that humor, we have been better able filter the coexisting feelings of awkwardness and shame that come with taking a tumble.

P.S.S. Questions and Activities for You (and Your Parents Too)

1. Ask your parents to tell you about their most embarrassing moment. How did they handle it?

2. Describe your funniest or most spectacular slip, trip, or fall!

3. Draw the experience!

Ah, Coffee!

Out of Mom's mouth came one tiny word
It was all that she said—all that was heard
Coffee, she uttered. It was quiet and muffled
Said as she sleepily stumbled and shuffled
Normally charming, but in the A.M. alarming
I did not even think as I made her that drink!
I said *Look at that hair! Did you sleep upside down?*
COFFEE, she sputtered, *NOW!* with a frown
Clink, clink, clink went her spoon as she stewed
Showing impatience while it was brewed
From our kitchen clock came the constant *tick-tock*
Although time seemed stilled while the coffee pot filled
As the lofty aroma wafted rich from those beans
The liquid gold had escaped, and at last meant caffeine
But her mug was held in a tight morning grasp
So I had to release that white-knuckled clasp
To gallantly pour the thing she adored
Right to the brim of her coffee cup's rim
With cream and sugar, made light and sweet
Always for her it was *my* morning treat
After one single sip, her morning had bloomed
Before the next one—*Ahhhhh, coffee*, she crooned
Now for a pit stop once she drained the last drop
She ran for the door while I brewed up some more!

P.S. I wrote this as a poem in tribute to those warm traditions that bring families together.

As a child, I had a wonderful game I played with my grandfather any time we went out to eat. Our game board was any restaurant table, and the pieces his coffee cup and the little creamer singles we called "mini moos." He would peel back a tiny edge of the creamers and ask, "Who wants to milk the cow?" Of course, I did! I would gently squeeze the "mini moo" just as if it were a teeny-tiny udder, making it look like I was milking a cow right into his coffee cup!

When I became a parent, my children not only "milked the cow," but brewed my morning coffee for me! After it was brewed and I took my first sip, we all sighed together: "Ahhhh, coffee!" We are such a coffee family that one day, my niece asked if I went to bed already thinking about the coffee I would have when I woke up! She started drinking her "coffee-milk" at the tender age of three, and as she got older, she also made coffee for her mother. When I visit, she will still make coffee for her Auntie B. Her sweet tradition warms my heart.

P.S.S. Questions and Activities for You (and Your Parents Too)

1. What is something special that you like to do to warm the heart of someone you love?

2. What is your favorite drink? What memories do you associate with it?

3. Draw a picture of that special drink; or, draw a picture representing something special you do to warm a loved one's heart.

_____

_____

_____

_____

_____

_____

_____

_____

_____

_____

_____

_____

_____

_____

_____

_____

_____

How to Haiku

This poem holds clues
To the pattern in haiku
They are meant for you

Three lines in a row
Syllables begin to flow
One more hint to know

Start with only five
Then seven chases the lot
Five a parting shot

Must a haiku rhyme?
It can if you're so inclined
Maybe this last time!

Now grab your pencil
Let the brainstorming begin
Your haiku awaits!

P.S. This poem was born out of a challenge to write in the haiku form. At first, I found it very difficult. In fact, I thought about giving up. I thought, I can't get my timing, I can't find a rhyme, arrrgh! It was time for super-breath!

I used my breath to stay calm, looked up authors who had written haikus, and plugged away. Little by little, I got the hang of the unique style, and the more I did, the more I enjoyed it!

As you can see, a haiku has three lines. The first line is five syllables long; the second has seven, and the third returns to five syllables. In bringing mindfulness into haiku, I decided to take five "haiku breaths" to begin the first five-syllable line. After that, I found myself counting the syllables on my fingers as I wrote. It was a totally engaging experience, and it was difficult to think of anything but writing as I was practicing.

When I wrote in haiku, I became totally lost in the creation of my little practice poems. I saw myself touching my fingers as I counted. I felt my fingers as I counted on them, and was thrilled when my syllables matched up! When I found myself frustrated, I returned to counting my breath. If I was on a five-syllable line, I counted five breaths. If I was on a seven-syllable line, I counted seven breaths. It worked really well.

I started writing haikus without including rhymes, mainly because if I thought about rhymes and counting syllables, I risked my head spinning so fast it might just fly up and off of my shoulders! I waited until I had mastered the syllable counts and when that fun was done, the rhymes came in time!

I found learning "how to Haiku" calming, and am glad to have been introduced to this little 5-7-5 gem. Let's see if you, too, can find the calmness of haiku.

P.S.S. Questions and Activities for You (and Your Parents Too)

1. Write about a time you were confronted with challenge.

2. Write three things you can do if you find yourself really frustrated with a task.

3. When is it okay to give up?

4. On your picture page, write and illustrate your own haiku! It can be about something you can see, or something that happened today, or even about reading poems! Start with five breaths, and go back to your breath if you start getting frustrated. Use finger-counting—and most of all, have fun!

GROW WITH ME POETRY

Write and illustrate your own haiku!

The Relay Race

The runners were ready, lined up toe to toe
One wavering gulp signaled *Ready—Set—Go!*
A checkered flush warmed, then appeared on my face
The flag had been waved, beginning the race
One tear welled, then sprinted from my eyelash
With two more following behind in a flash
In tandem flowing, with passion they ran
Down with speed, as only tears can
They streaked 'cross the finish, in an unbroken stream
Though a few lone stragglers were trailing the team
Until the track lay bare, no tears fell down my face
One heavy, long sigh marked the end of the race.
A bit out of breath, I sought out what was tufted
'Top the treasure chest holding the tissues I trusted
To clean up the remnants of the relay
And all that was left of my utter dismay
With a gentle blow and a soft dab to finish
The burst of emotion slowly diminished
My moment's sad relay race has been run
And so onward now; a new moment's begun.

P.S. I wrote this poem as I thought about the act of crying, and of those tears themselves. They are such fluid little creatures.

Crying is a common experience. I am an ugly crier: tears splotch and blotch my face, and when I am done I look like I could star in my own horror movie. But the funny thing is, I don't care. It makes me feel better. The splotches eventually fade back to my normal rosy complexion, and I simply consider myself to have been "moisturized." Sometimes you just need a good cry to release our feelings and feel rejuvenated.

Haven't you ever noticed how sometimes people will burst into tears upon seeing a loved one they haven't seen in years? Of course, these are tears of joy, just as sad tears may be shed at the thought of saying goodbye to this very same person. There are tears that come from pain (hitting your finger, instead of the nail, with a hammer), tears that come when we feel so icky we can't cope (the flu will do this for sure), tears that come after hearing a hilarious joke (haven't you ever laughed until you cried?), and tears that come from fear (after your sibling jumps out of the closet at you wearing a horrifying mask). These are all teary emotional releases. Finally, I've come to understand what I did not as a child: there is no shame in crying. We all need to cry, at any age. It's part of life. We live, we cry, and then we might even cry some more—and it is okay.

P.S.S. Questions and Activities for You (and Your Parents Too)

1. Write about the rules you think apply to when, where, and if you should cry.

2. Write about who you think made up those rules, and whether you think they are fair. What changes would you make to the "rules" of crying?

3. What are the sensations you feel in your body before you cry, and then after the tears have passed?

4. Draw a racetrack with tears running their "relay race."

Draw a racetrack with tears running their "relay race."

Abracadabra

I'm so angry, I just might yell!

Nothing on earth is going that well

I'm so out of sorts that I really might cry

I can't cheer myself up, no matter how hard I try

As I sit and I stew, I recall mood is contagious

So I decide to seek out someone wholly outrageous

I call my best friend to *catch* a new start

To see if a chat might help lighten my heart

Hello? There's a happiness there in her tone

I feel my mood lift as my ear cups the phone

Soon we are sharing a sweet belly laugh

Shedding enough silly tears to fill a warm bath

Giggling until I can stand it no more

I return to the person I was once before

Now with a big grin from left ear to right

I seek out another with no smile in sight

Beside them I'll sit, my silent wand waving

In truth, *abracadabra* is not so amazing

We all carry magic in the palm of our hand

Pixie dust to cast out in a fashion that's grand

So remember that whenever you see a frown

A bit of enchantment can turn it around.

P.S. This was written when I found myself in a horribly foul mood, beaten down by life. My situation was so bad, I didn't know whether to laugh or cry. So what does a girl do when she is mad? She calls her best friend. What do we learn from having someone else lift our spirits? Pay it forward! The next time you see a friend out of sorts, see if your voice might just cheer them up.

P.S.S. Questions and Activities for You (and Your Parents Too)

1. Who is your go-to person when you need a pick-me-up? Tell me about them!

2. What does this person say or do to make you happy when you feel sad? What do you say or do to cheer up someone who is feeling blue?

3. Describe how you feel after you are responsible for making someone else feel better. Does it affect you in any way? If so, how?

4. Draw a collage of all the things that make you happy when you are sad; or if you like, draw a magic wand, or pixie dust being sprinkled from an open hand!

Speak Up and Take Your Place in This World

Wear this or wear that on this special day

Or be cast aside without the slightest delay

To set aside your unease both within and without

Is to resign like a lemming to the sea despite doubt

To partake in what others tell you you must

Is to ignore the compass in your heart that you trust

In the background is a whisper that quietly pleads

    Take hold of the reins and command your own lead!

As your inner whisper becomes a great shout

It will guide you safely down your perfect route

It bids you to

    Speak up and take your place in this world!

Even if the scuttlebutt about you still swirls

You can always break free from the chains that bind you

Your conscience being what you strive to live up to

Like a bird in the wind, your courage will soar

As the cowardly lion rears back now and roars

And then—guess what—and this is the gem

Never again will you want to be "them"!

P.S. My grandmother repeated one story over and over in her later years. She had been a timid child, and one day, in the hallway of her school, the principal stopped her and said, "Blanchie, speak up and take your place in this world." It was a powerful message, and as she repeated it, she impressed that message upon others. This was her legacy, her gift to us; and now it is my gift to you.

P.S.S. Questions and Activities for You (and Your Parents Too)

1. When have you been called to speak up?

2. When should you speak up?

3. How do you feel when you do speak up. How do you feel when you don't?

4. Draw and blend all the colors that make you think of courage. Look at your drawing after you've finished. Does it make you feel strong?

The Assembly

As the guest speaker at your school
There is a fire I'd like to fuel
Raise one hand high in the air
If anyone's ever made fun of your hair
Or the way that you talk, or the things that you like
Or if you've rudely been told to *butt out, take a hike!*
Wiggle your fingers if you've ever felt fear
Or dread at the start of each day of the year
Do tales of you float around in cyberspace?
Or pictures you find that you just can't erase?
Now raise up your hand if you've ever found humor
In belittling another or in spreading a rumor
Have you ever wondered just what makes you tick?
Why attacking another is your only joystick?
Look at those fingers wave high in the air
Is the world where we live one where nobody cares?

Both bully and bullied are in need of advice
For there is a reason for each to think twice
The bullied must know their secret causes more harm
Than what happens the day after they sound the alarm
The bully must learn that way deep down under
A great storm is brewing with lightning and thunder
Atop both of your heads, you'll see those dark clouds loom
And they'll never be quelled within your bedroom
To the bullied who weeps, now hear this you must:
You do have a voice, listen to it and trust
To the bully it's time now to listen up please:
This thing that you have is like a silent disease
Without quarantine it will rapidly spread
Leaving you unprepared for the future ahead
Every mean act is a door slammed on your cell

A cold lonely place where only you dwell
Cast there by all those who in a fit of great pique
Found your justice and honor to be woefully weak
But still there is hope for the two of you in your plight
If only one speaks out and the other ceases to fight
Believe in yourself this above all:
You *both* are important, so stand proud and tall
To those in the crowd whose hands have stayed down
Were you ever the witness who uttered no sound?
Scared the next target might just be you
Did you turn a blind eye while bidding adieu?
If so, put your right hand over your heart
And repeat these last words before we part:
Today my head will come out of the sand
I vow now to lend my neighbor a hand
Never again will I stand by and be daunted
And watch while another is brutally taunted
Now cup your hands to both of your ears
To make these last words of mine easy to hear:
A heart is fragile and easily broken
Just as it is mended by words that are spoken.

P.S. I wrote this poem after turning on the nightly news only to hear two adults belittling each other. I noticed that they chose words that bullies are also often very fond of (E.g., stupid, ignorant, dumb). They even used intimidating nonverbal language common to bullies (eye-rolling, finger pointing, loud angry tones). The spectacle made me want to impress how important it is to have an open dialogue about such behavior and to nip it in the bud!

I was not bullied frequently as a child. However, the few times I was stood out to the point of imprinting memories and sensations. In one grammar-school incident, I had been following a gaggle of students down a double-wide staircase. I still remember the smell of new rubber tread on the stairs comingled with the odor of sweaty boys who had just run in from recess. I felt tiny compared to the older kids that swarmed around me, and I remember how their laughter rang out and echoed as they reached for me and shoved my third-grade self right down the flight of stairs. Confused and scared, I tumbled and landed heavily on my knees. Why had they done such a hateful thing? And would they find me later and do it again?

They never returned, and I was lucky not to be plagued by bullies growing up. But how amazing that my middle-aged self can remember that fear so vividly.

I have actually encountered more bullies in the adult world then I did as a child. Nowadays, I am better equipped to deal with their behavior, but I believe that childhood bullies left unchecked turn into manipulative, gossiping, catty, power-hungry, overbearing peers, bosses, and even world leaders. Simply put, they become the bullies of the adult world. This cycle must stop.

Take a moment and decide where you fall in the bully cycle. Be honest with yourself, and remember that you first have to acknowledge a behavior if you want to change it.

P.S.S. Questions and Activities for You (and Your Parents Too)

1. Start a conversation with your parent(s) by asking them what they think bullying actually is. Then share your own opinions on the subject (they could be very different!).

2. These next questions are hard, but important. Ask your parent to consider if they have ever bullied anyone or watched anyone be bullied without doing anything. Now, you consider the same questions and open an honest dialogue about that situation. If you do not feel you can start the conversation, write down what you would like to say and then ask a parent to read what you have written. This can help start your conversation. They can do the same!

3. Ask your parent if they were ever bullied. If they were, how did they manage the situation. Looking back, would they handle it differently?

4. Have you ever been bullied? Does it happen often? How? Talk to your parents about this situation. If you feel you can't, again, write down what is happening to you and then invite your parent or another important adult in your life to read what you have written.

5. Draw a bully, or fill the page with colors that blend together to represent the way a bully can make you feel.

GROW WITH ME POETRY

Draw a bully, or fill the page with colors that blend together to represent the way a bully can make you feel.

Moby Rich

Near the coast of New Jersey, a man roams the bay
Fish quake at the sight of him, legend does say
Like a beacon, his snowy hair lights up the night
For those few who might spot him, to their delight
Dodging whitecaps and buoys with hardly a worry
(For unlike ol' Ahab, he holds no great fury)
As swiftly he casts out a very long line
If no fish are caught, it would all be just fine
Unconcerned if there's nary a minnow to cook
He would just have more time to read a good book
And who would know? since all fishermen say
I hooked me a big one, but it done got away!

P.S. My father is a humble fisherman—or are the fish humbled by him? This poem is a tribute to him and the funny, kind, and smart fisherman he truly is. By the way, his name is "Richard." The title of this poem was simply the icing on the cake!

P.S.S. Questions and Activities for You (and Your Parents Too)

1. Describe your father or mentor. What are his good qualities? What are his less-good qualities? (We all have them.) Ask your parent to describe their father figure.

2. What makes a good father? What are a father's responsibilities?

3. Draw a picture of him; or if you would like, draw a picture of how you envision Moby Rich. He would consider it an honor!

Road Signs

They come in yellow and in white
Sometimes orange and sometimes red
They do not glow in the daylight
But in the dark instead.

The orange blaze of a *detour* sign
Disrupts your chosen route
Forcing you now to realign
Like an ant trailing blindly about.

The *hazard* and the *caution* signs
Can each give you an awful scare
For what lurks ahead might just define
Your next sharp turn RIGHT THERE!

Don't get me started on the *Yields*
As clumps of cars blow by en masse
Look at me behind my windshield
Why won't you let me pass?

Now and again there's a four way *stop*
Rules in place for who may next proceed
But when some tool pulls off a swap
A curse goes forth with speed!

The *Round-a-bout* sign is a carnival wonder
With cars spinning on a carousel
So many exits, but if you blunder
It's a circle! So all is well.

Oops! I missed the *speed limit* sign!
Blue flashing lights call me to stop
Thank heavens—a warning and not a fine
How I could kiss that cop!

I spy a little *rest area* sign
A potty break we must allow
Pit stop done, then comes a whine
Are we there yet? Not long now.

WHAT? *Dead End?* No, not that sign!
I'm dejected and totally perplexed
A forced K-turn, back down the line
At least I know what's next

More road signs and re-navigation
'Til at last, *You have reached your destination.*

P.S. We all face difficult times in our lives, and in this poem, they come in the form of "road signs." Even if you don't drive yourself, you have definitely been in the car with someone who has gotten lost after taking a detour! I venture to guess that all of us have taken a road trip that did not go quite as planned, and the road signs along the way played their part in its going awry. This poem speaks to something we can all relate to: annoying road signs and how they derail our journey. It is comforting to know that we can grow stronger from adversity. I take care in suggesting that even if you do not come out unscathed from your life's tribulations, you will be better able to navigate the next hazard sign along your journey.

P.S.S. Questions and Activities for You (and Your Parents Too)

1. What was the last difficult situation you faced in your life?

2. How have you grown from this experience?

3. What are you better at now, because you navigated through this adversity?

4. Road signs tell us when to stop or go, when to wait for others, when to retrace our steps, or when to take a break. Think about life's road signs. Draw the one that you are best at managing and the one you have the most trouble managing. Make sure to label them!

Mirror, Mirror

Look in the mirror, and what should I see?
The obvious answer is that I'll see me!
But I have a secret, a fun one indeed
To look in that mirror, I have no need
As I repeat the old riddle, I pretend to be bold
Though what answer I get might just be "two" fold
I say, *Mirror, Mirror, now up on my wall,*
Is there another who is fairest of all?
Your sister, you silly! Of course you have seen
Two mirror images with no glass in between
How, you might ask me, *can that be true?*
Unless, by golly, there are two of you!
TWINS indeed, right from the start
Another from whom I could never part
Though at times I wonder, *What's up with the stare?*

Forgetting the spellbinding face that I share
To embrace what's unique both inside and out
Is what life as a twin has been all about
Into my reflection now I speak as I gaze
At my sister staring back at me straight through the haze
Mirror, O Mirror, who is the fairest you see
Before you now? Do you have an answer for me?
A voice was heard without the slightest delay
As my mirror, in parting, had these words to relay
Child, O child before me I see
A beautiful you, and a most lovely she
With that, I gave the reflection a kiss
And with it I fondly did reminisce
Of the magical bond that grew from within
The day I was born alongside a twin.

P.S. I was blessed to be born with an identical twin, and I wrote this poem as a tribute to her and the giggles we can't help but share as we walk side by side.

As much as I enjoy being a twin, it's made me notice that while we teach our children not to stare, people often fail to follow that rule when it comes to "look-alikes." This "don't stare" rule has good intentions. It's meant to teach sympathy and keeps us from unintentionally hurting one another's feelings. If we stare at a person who looks or acts differently, it may make that person feel self-conscious about being different. But in doing so, the "don't stare" lesson inadvertently teaches an unintended lesson: to ignore those who are different. My solution when my children were growing up was to teach them that, if you are going to stare, you have to wave and say hello! In doing so, you have shown that you value this person just as much as any other person, and to boot, have also shown them that they too deserve your attention and kindness, not because they are different, but because they are individuals just like you and me—and in my case, my twin.

Over time, I came to understand why people did a reflexive double-take upon actually seeing double, and I now find tremendous humor in the inevitable confusion the world feels upon seeing us together. This poem was born from a life of eyes boring a hole through me, and answers the simple question everyone needs to ask: Are you twins?

P.S.S. Questions and Activities for You (and Your Parents Too)

1. Have you ever been stared at? Why do you think that was?

2. How did it make you feel?

3. How do you think it would make a person feel if you said Hello after you met their gaze?

4. Draw a pair of eyes staring.

Draw a pair of eyes staring.

A Midnight Flight

I wonder sometimes
If the sound that you first heard
Could've been that bird

His bundle in tow
The legendary stork flew
Through the midnight hue

My aviator
In smooth determination
Sought out his vision

One destination
Where his flight slowed to a stop
And with it—a drop!

Now within his sights
A smile crept across his beak
Then grew cheek to cheek

The night air in tow
My blanket cast up and 'round
Parachuted down

Into a cradle
Landed those ten teensie toes
Lit by a halo

I thank my mail-bird
Recalling that moonlit night
And my stork in flight

Hope's bundle of joy
In its wake hid a white dove
And heavenly love

With a soft slow blink
Our longing hearts skipped a beat
As our eyes did meet

In that one moment
I swore I heard my bird say
It's adoption day!

So now hear *my* words
Ringing soundly from my voice
You too were my choice.

P.S. Everyone knows about the Stork. His legend lives on in those giant signs planted in front yards, announcing to the world that a new baby has arrived. But while I knew how the Stork delivered my children to my home, after writing "XX" and "XY," I wondered how he delivered adopted babies to their new families. How did I find out? A really big birdie whispered in my ear! He inspired me to write about the bond between adopted children and their parents.

Children are adopted under all kinds of circumstances and for all kinds of reasons, but whatever their stories, to be part of a family who chose each other is something truly special. So for all the adopted children in the world, and all the children still waiting to find their families, I want to remind you how much you matter, and with care, point out that loving homes come in as many shapes and sizes as the children that fill them.

P.S.S. Questions and Activities for You (and Your Parents Too)

1. Have your parents or foster parents tell you about the day they brought you home.

If you have not yet been adopted or found a foster home, describe the kind of home and family you would like to find.

If you would prefer, describe that special person who you yourself have adopted as your parent.

If you live with your biological parents, what do you think it might be like for a child to have adoptive or foster parents?

2. Write three things about yourself that "glow"—things that make you stand out in a good way!

3. Draw a big stork flying with a baby in tow!

Draw a big stork flying with a baby in tow!

Stop This Ride

Stop this roller coaster, I want to get off!
I've had quite enough of these steep hills and troughs
With the dizzying speed at which it flies around
It must surely have broken the speed of sound!
Didn't I tell you that heights make me shiver?
And each plunge down makes my whole body quiver!
From the start to the finish and the top to the drop
Wondering when, oh when will it stop?
Whipping around now at each twist and each turn
No control to be had, just one lesson to learn
Some things are fun only after they're scary
So give it a whirl even though you are wary

Of the *tick-tick-tick-ticking* that carts you up high
Or the startling drops that bring tears to your eye
From zero to sixty in a New York minute
The ride will be over and you can boast at the finish
It's not just a ride, but how we go through life
Staying the course, no matter the strife
We all want to stop at times on the way
But we bought the ticket, and now we must stay
So hold on my friends, and soon you will find
The final curve's near, the worst is behind
Relief washes over as the ride slows back down
Your smile grows wider as your feet touch the ground
Now make for the exit, still beaming with pride
For you faced your fear and finished that ride!

P.S. This poem speaks of those times when life "gives you lemons." However, sometimes life is just so bad you can't even make a decent pitcher of lemonade. This poem is for those times when you want to give up and dump the whole thing down the sink. It's important to know that your struggles, whatever they are, are real and valid. But it is equally important to know that they will end, and that when they do, you will be proud to have survived the ride amid all those sour lemons.

P.S.S. Questions and Activities for You (and Your Parents Too)

1. Write about something that is overwhelming you. What can you do about it?

2. Draw a picture of a super imaginative roller coaster!

Draw a picture of a super imaginative roller coaster!

"Buddy"

Husband, father, and friend so tall
A prize of a person even when he felt small
For a man of few words, he said so very much
Loving and kind, with a soft tender touch
Values upheld and shared from the start
How are y'all? spoken, true to the heart
He held onto this life though nudged forth to another
Filled with light and heavenly wonder
Husband, father, and friend, he'll be missed
Gotta go, in his words, sealed with a kiss.

P.S. I wrote this poem in memory of an old-fashioned southern gentleman. He was a wonderful father and fantastic "Paw-Paw." For as long as I knew him, he loved to visit, but would always get up within thirty minutes, exclaiming, "Gotta go!" He was a strong, independent man until his final months, when his body and mind succumbed to illness. In his last days, when he was unable to talk, he would simply wave or blow you a kiss. This poem was written in loving remembrance.

P.S.S. Questions and Activities for You (and Your Parents Too)

1. Did you notice a trend in "Buddy's" personality? What do you think his values were in life?

2. What is your "Paw-Paw" like? What makes him special?

3. Draw a picture of your "Paw-Paw." If he is not living, let your parent tell you about him, and then draw a picture of how you see him in your head! If you don't want to draw, make a word collage that represents this grandparent.

GROW WITH ME POETRY

Kissing Frogs

I set out to marry the girl of my dreams
Yet to my despair, it was not meant to be
Thanks to these pesky issues: my age and dumb genes
She was my mommy, and I was just three!

At five, my heart was set all aflutter
With a super girl who was not my mommy
But she pined for jelly with peanut butter
And I only loved cheese and salami.

I became smitten again as a tween
Behind her glasses were eyes ocean blue
Why couldn't I even make myself seen?
Sadly, it would never be me that she knew.

A cheerleader made my insides cartwheel
She was the star of the halftime show
I asked her out, telling her how I did feel
But she clapped her hands and chanted N-O!

Many years later, as I hopped along
Covered in warts and dripping in slime
I heard my princess's sweet soft song
And I knew she was meant to be mine.

Now dressed in white, she stands before me
I shed one tear as I wait up ahead
As we both speak, *I now take thee*
Our fairytale ending when *I do's* are said.

My love had the courage to kiss this poor frog
So that we two could be joyfully wed
A fine lesson croaked to a toad on a log
Hippity-hop, for up there ahead

Your princess too awaits noble bliss
As she searches for a frog prince to kiss.

P.S. It seems we always hear about the princess and her journey, but never the frog. I wanted to retell this familiar story from his perspective, and found a fun and meaningful way to put a new spin on an age-old adage.

Whether we are the frog prince or the princess, we all long for true love. I didn't think I would ever find the "love of my life," but one day there he was: my frog prince. We have been married for almost thirty years. He and I both kissed a few frogs before finding each other, and we both thought that some of those frogs were going to be the people we would spend the rest of our lives with.

We are lucky to have very fond memories of the people we dated before meeting each other, but we also have memories of heartbreak. Hearts can break at any age. I wrote this poem as I remembered my childhood crushes, as well as my own children's experiences with love. I watched the utter elation as they found happiness in people they could unravel with, and then sorrow as those people later asked them to be someone they could not, or were not ready to be. They searched, they morphed, they tried on personalities, and then settled into the souls they were meant to be, warts and all.

A broken or yearning heart is the heart that falls prey to the perils of love. Use this poem to open a dialogue with your parents about relationships—and more importantly, about healthy relationships.

P.S.S. Questions and Activities for You (and Your Parents Too)

1. Think about what makes relationships successful and what makes them fail. This may be a good time to ask your parents for their opinion! Write down the highlights from your discussion.

2. Discuss healthy ways to handle a broken heart (this would be another good time for parental input!).

3. Make a list of "Deal Breakers" (issues that should immediately end a relationship).

4. List five traits you want your frog prince or princess to have, and five traits you could do without!

5. Draw a frog prince or frog princess!

GROW WITH ME POETRY

Draw a frog prince or frog princess!

WAIT! You Matter

There's a place in this world for each of our hearts
Even though there are some who may wish to depart
Fallen into a pit of despair
Convinced that no one can understand them or care
Hearing a voice that they must set aside
Which asks them to seek out a heavenly ride
Missing the flint to re-ignite and begin
Unable to spark their own flame from within
To stoke what smolders, you must poke the ember
That lucent red coal at your spirit's center
Now gather your anguish and set it ablaze
The billowing smoke is a victory haze
Each second that passes, a battle is won
So bask in the glory, then fight the next one
Reach out your hand for any to hold
And within that grasp, new hope will unfold
As your bonfire's warmth is felt through and through
Remember, *YOU MATTER*—there is no one like you!

P.S. I wrote this hoping that my words might touch at least one person and inspire them to seek guidance in a time of desperate need. Why? Because the world is a better place with you in it.

If you or a loved one is in need, there are many forms of help out there, such as the National Suicide Prevention Lifeline at 1-800-273-TALK (8255), or IMALIVE.org. These are just two of the many resources available to assist you, and provide immediate access to "talk" or "chat," respectively.

P.S.S. Questions and Activities for You (and Your Parent Too)

1. Kids, this might be a difficult conversation, but ask you parents if they know anyone who suffers from depression or anxiety. Ask if they mind talking about your family history, and learn about the mental health of your own family tree. Write down what it felt like to talk about such an "adult" topic with your parents.

2. Take some time to consider your own emotions. Everyone gets sad or nervous sometimes, but it is the more extreme emotions that tell us we might need help. Think of physical health for a moment. A little runny nose might just be the common cold. But add body aches, a terrible cough, a hundred-and-three-degree fever—well, a doctor's appointment might be in order! Your emotional health is no different: a little sadness here, some butterflies there, and some simple mood swings might be part of everyday tween or teenage angst. But when those feeling become overwhelming, much like the case of a high fever, it might be time to ask for help. If you are feeling overwhelmed by negative feelings, it may be a good time to talk to your parents or another adult you trust. Show them this entry and try talking things through, even though it may be difficult. If you are unable to think of anyone you could talk to, remember you can use one of the services listed above to chat with an anonymous person about what you are holding close to your heart. There is always someone out there who cares!

3. Within a star, blend together the colors that represent your current mood. If you don't like that mood, follow up this drawing with another star that blends together the colors that represent the mood you would like to have.

When I Am Older

When I am older, what should I be?
So many choices that I can see
Therapist, mechanic—should I try college, I wonder?
It's far too much pressure, I'm buckling under!
I can be anything to which I put my mind
But if I don't decide soon, I'll get left behind!
And if I don't succeed, just what happens then?
Can I go back in time and start over again?
I can't even move, I'm so very afraid
Of finding a mistake in the choices I've made
So when I get older there is just one thing
A thought and a mantra, to which I will cling
Nothing is certain, nor set ever in stone
As many before me so kindly have shown
In my own good time, I will figure it out
My one destined path, I haven't a doubt
So now when I wonder just what I should be
I know all I need do is simply be me.

P.S. "Analysis paralysis" happens when you spend so long thinking over a decision that you start worrying about all the ways each possibility could go wrong, until your thought process spirals out of control and leaves you unable to make any decision at all.

Every young adult is confronted with the question, "What do you want to be when you grow up?" The answers are so simple at first: "I want to be Daddy," then "I want to be a star," and finally, "I want to help people." Around eighth or ninth grade, the churning begins, followed by worry, and then paralysis. I wrote this poem for all those heading for, or already caught in, that trap. In a world where so much value is placed on our occupation, I felt the need to go back to our roots, and remind anyone reading this that who you are is more important than what you do.

P.S.S. Questions and Activities for You (and Your Parents Too)

1. What do you like to learn about? What types of occupations relate to what you like to learn?

2. Think of the people you look up to. What are their occupations?

3. Draw a picture of something that represents what you might like to be when you are older; or, if you already have an idea, draw a picture of different items used by people in that career.

The Egg and I

Humpty Dumpty was decidedly grumpy

His fall off the wall was a little too bumpy!

Not being hardboiled, left oozing and runny

Yolk seeping through cracks, he was no longer sunny

As he lay splayed out, his ripples not still

Though broken he yet found inside him the will

Now back in his egg cup, half-full it did seem

Not yet half-empty, he dreamed up a dream

He spread his white wings and slowly did amble

And in all of his glory, turned a deep amber scramble.

GROW WITH ME POETRY

P.S. "The Egg and I" is more than a simple nursery rhyme. It's about many things: grumpiness, accidents, death, the afterlife, and most of all, the power of positivity. This is a poem that will mean different things to different people.

I fell in love with the idea of a grumpy soul finding his will to turn something seemingly tragic into a fairytale ending. For Humpty Dumpty, even though one event changed him forever, who or what he became—though changed—was still beautiful.

P.S.S. Questions and Activities for You (and Your Parents Too)

1. What does this poem mean to you?

2. Draw Humpty Dumpty as you like to see him.

Draw Humpty Dumpty as you like to see him.

"ing"

Looking, looking, looking
trying to see what is to be
Running, running, running
when we feel so out of control
Hiding, hiding, hiding
leaves us stranded within our thoughts
Wondering, wondering, wondering
why do I feel so terribly lost?
Knowing, knowing, knowing
sometimes there are no answers
Mourning, mourning, mourning
what we may never know
Reaping, reaping, reaping
the rewards that come from trying
Sowing, sowing, sowing
that glowing silver lining
Shining, shining, shining
beyond the pain of pining.

P.S. This poem was written for a very special someone who shared a secret with me. Everyone has secrets, and they are often too painful to be ignored. We all deserve to move through and past them, and finally past our own judgement of what we have hidden.

P.S.S. Questions and Activities for You (and Your Parents Too)

1. Do you have a secret? Start a dialogue with your parent or another trusted adult about this topic.

2. When is it okay to divulge a secret?

3. How does keeping a secret make us feel?

4. What do you think happens to your body physically when you keep a secret? (E.g., can it make you feel agitated or tired?) If you are not sure, this would be a question to ask your parents!

5. Draw a secret locked inside a box.

GROW WITH ME POETRY

Draw a secret locked inside a box.

Enlightened Me

I'm not quite the same as I was yesterday
The world's opened up in a very strange way
I feel as if I am a single round peg
Forced in a square hole, no room for one leg
Experiencing something that sets you apart
Something you know to be real in your heart
Builds a steady unease that can burn
     through and through
Chipping away at all you once thought to be true
You'll discover your peace as your spirit speaks out
It just takes a whisper, there's no need to shout
To learn it's the path that matters much more
Than where you wind up, or why and what for
Follow the light deep within who you are
For you—you alone—are your own shining star.

P.S. When you "see the light," that light can take many forms. It can seem as if you are walking around with your own little spotlight following you around, pointing out to one and all, "Look at me, I am different!" Of course, this is just your mind playing tricks on you, making you feel that all eyes are upon you.

This poem was written for those out there who feel just a little bit different, and need to embrace the light that shines within in order to accept what that light reveals.

P.S.S. Questions and Activities for You (and Your Parents Too)

1. In what ways do you feel that you are "different"?

2. How have you embraced that difference?

3. How do you treat someone else that seems "different"? Be truthful with yourself.

4. Draw a shining star. Make it your own! Maybe draw yourself under a spotlight. If you would like, a combination; a star under a spotlight!

Nil

Why is it so hard to turn down the sound?
To be alone with your thoughts with no noises around
That daily barrage of distractions repeated
All that ambient noise that can leave us depleted
Do we fear what we'll hear when at last we are still?
That the voice in our heads will be piercing and shrill?
Such thoughts are deserving of hushed contemplation
A nice peaceful spot is an ideal location
To take time out to listen, and soon you will find
Insight, resolve, and presence of mind
Beautiful music lies beyond what you hear
A harmony of sorts, resoundingly clear
With a decrescendo gently falling within
As all of your thoughts are now ceasing to spin
An enticing gift to unwrap if you will
Given to those who seek peace within nil.

P.S. I wrote this poem while thinking about silence and wondering why we resist it with such fervor. For years my mother told me, "You should really try meditation, it is very calming." For a long time, she had watched me struggle unsuccessfully to outrun a black cloud that rained misfortune after misfortune on my and my family's heads. Over two decades or so, we had faced a childhood brain tumor (thankfully benign, but terrifying nonetheless), chronic illness, assault, and bitter injustice; and through it all, I was fighting to balance marriage, motherhood, and a demanding (albeit rewarding) career. I hardly had time to cry, let alone meditate. But when at last I was overcome, and the tears just wouldn't stop, all that was left was my mother's advice.

I really hate when my mother is right, yet she was. I came to love meditation. Do you know what happens during meditation? Nothing. Eventually the world stops, and it feels like you are floating on top of the black cloud, not trapped beneath it. It is peace. The sound of silence is beautiful. Trust me; I too am a mother, and mothers are always right.

P.S.S. Questions and Activities for You (and Your Parents Too)

1. Does your mind feel busy? Name one thing you could cut out of your schedule to give yourself some more quiet time.

2. If you don't like the quiet, why do you think that is?

3. What do you hear when it is quiet?

Exercise: Set a timer for one minute. While the clock ticks, just sit and listen to your breath go in and out. What else did you hear other than your breath? Use your imagination and listen. Increase the duration of the exercise as you begin to relax and enjoy your introduction to meditation.

4. Blend together various colors that feel calming to you. Let the colors fill the page.

The Power

How can one little feeling hold such great power
Like the winds of a storm, make us huddle and cower?
So frozen within, right down to the bone
Feeling so helplessly cold and alone
In pity and wariness, totally knowing
We alone hold the hoe to the row we are sowing
So try it right now, to be totally still
For deep down inside is the calmness of will
Find the kaleidoscope behind each closed eye
Colors and patterns to watch as you lie
Feel the winds turn to a tepid calm breeze
Now breathing deeply and fairly at ease
The angst that still lingers will trickle away
That powerful feeling conquered today
Though the final step in gaining control
Is to seek out and grasp what has taken its toll
Label what was and why it took hold
Then toss it away, for the truth has been told
No need to revisit what stirred up the dust
Return to yourself, and yourself you must trust
Let go of the past and live for what is
No turning back, now let go and forgive.

P.S. This poem is about emotion—specifically, panic. It defines the feeling itself, our role in taking control of it, and most importantly, the need to avoid judging ourselves for having experienced it. Even if you haven't experienced a panic attack personally, it's likely that someone you know has. Panic is all-encompassing and destructive, but with patience and care, it can be managed.

P.S.S. Questions and Activities for You (and Your Parents Too)

1. What do you feel when you're nervous?

2. What do you do when you feel nervous?

3. When is it normal to feel nervous, and when are you letting your nerves get the best of you? Discuss this topic with your parents!

4. Draw a picture of what it feels like to be nervous. Maybe a picture of a big belly with butterflies swirling around inside of it. Or maybe a picture of something that has a "pit," like a well or a giant hole. In this hole, blend the colors that you feel represent nervousness.

Draw a picture of what it feels like to be nervous. Maybe a picture of a big belly with butterflies swirling around inside of it.

Or maybe a picture of something that has a "pit," like a well or a giant hole. In this hole, blend the colors that you feel represent nervousness.

It Could be You

Goldilocks slept in a bed *juuust* right
And awoke to three bears coming home for the night!
Snow White, so fair, ate a ruby-red gem
From an evil old witch she mistook for a friend
And those three little pigs, well they were all a bit lazy
To ignore the wolf's huffing and puffing was crazy
(Little Red Riding Hood, in her defense
Knew that the wolf was spewing nonsense)
The swine, Goldilocks, little Red, and Snow White
All missed the moral underwriting their plight
Consider perhaps it rings differently though
Than what you may think that you already know
Poor Goldilocks risked a terrible fate
And so did Snow White with the apple she ate
Those fat strips of bacon lost their humble abodes
Their error in judgment not building to code
Learn from them yes, but make no mistake
For here is another simple keepsake
Don't cast stones or join with a jury
Quick to lay blame in a judgmental fury
For as the world spins and all in due time
You too may appear in your own nursery rhyme.

P.S. Sometimes a poem comes from a single thought. The one that sparked this poem was, "How can I write a poem including nursery rhymes and children's classic stories?" I wondered how I could wrap all the classic morals into another common one and then condense the concept into a poem.

The common moral I chose was important to me. In my life I have come to feel that the word "never" should be eliminated from everyone's vocabulary. The idea that "I would never...!" and "It could never...!" are laden with such inherent judgement that, in holding such beliefs, you lose your ability to sympathize with those who are most in need of your compassion. As life would have it, you may just set yourself up not only to sympathize, but to truly empathize with the very same people you judged, because you never thought you would be in their shoes. Mistakes happen, and we will falter. No one is perfect, right? Like Snow White, we will all take that forbidden apple at one point or another and suffer the consequences. It is in those moments that we seek the compassion of others, and find ourselves remembering with embarrassment all the times we thought, 'I would never have done something like that!'

P.S.S. Questions and Activities for You (and Your Parents Too)

1. When was the last time you felt judged, or judged someone else for something they did? How did it make you (or them) feel?

2. Have you or a friend ever done one thing that changed the course of your life? If so, what?

3. What is your favorite nursery rhyme or children's book? Why?

4. Draw a picture of a character from your favorite nursery rhyme.

Save Your Self

Tepid and wilted, now truly fainthearted
Riddled with caution because we parted
From truths we once thought to be set in stone
Now separated, we feel quite alone
A view far from ours, although no less real
If held by a stranger is no great ordeal
But woe to our soul when the sentiment there
Is held by the one for whom you most care
Grief, disappointment, sadness, and ire
Can lead down a path that soon will require
A repair to the fracture before it can spread
Spidering out like a web in your head
But why hold another's opinion so dear?
Is it really the loss of our truths that we fear?
A war of this sort might be won at great cost
But your own sense of self will surely be lost
So think 'til you feel smoke come out of your ears
Is your self-esteem worth giving in to your fears?
Your foundation is strong—it was built long ago
To survive when the earth shudders deep down below.

P.S. I wrote this poem during a time when I was questioning what it took to keep my sense of self intact. It seems human nature has tied our self-esteem to how those around us feel about what we believe. I'd like to think that if our foundations are strong, our own senses of self can withstand differing opinions. However, even the strongest foundations can crumble if we are constantly forced to defend the opinions and truths we hold dear. Maybe if we label what we really fear, we would be more able to live and let live, as long as we don't lose our "selves" in the process.

P.S.S. Questions and Activities for You (and Your Parents Too)

1. Whose opinion do you care about the most?

2. Why do you think their opinion matters to you so much?

3. What is self-esteem? Do you think you have good self-esteem?

4. Write or draw a word or picture collage of at least five things you are good at.

Write or draw a word or picture collage of at least five things you are good at.

Big Worry Words

Winds full of fury, thoughts filled with fire
Whirling words lost in a silent quagmire
Wavelets and white caps, then a great tidal wave
Perilous waters that soon will enslave
That which is chained in the depth of our being
Circumlocutions, a tornado we're seeing
To dwell on *perhaps*, not forgetting *what if*
May leave you unable to see today's gifts
True, ominous clouds may be coming your way
But the storm you create you can just blow away
The sea looks like glass before lightning and thunder
Let that be your clue, seize the moment and wonder
Does worry define what it is you *might* see
Instead of the truth of all that *will* be?

P.S. I wrote this poem to validate the feelings of worry, but also to highlight the peril of succumbing to those feelings that each and every one of us has had to navigate.

Worry is inherently silent and full of unrest. It breeds exhaustion, both emotional and physical—the same exhaustion that perpetuates our inability to see what is real. When we slip into this distorted perception, we risk becoming defined by our worry. How can we ever see the little gems in life if we live shaken and shattered?

This is another moment to stress the importance of mindfulness, because if we become skilled in paying attention to what is happening in the moment, we can steer our minds away from what we are worried about, knowing that almost all worries revolve around what has yet to happen.

P.S.S. Questions and Activities for You (and Your Parents Too)

1. Are you a worrier?

2. What do you do when you worry?

3. Name one thing you can do to keep yourself from being overcome with worry. If you need a reminder, this would be a great time to reread "A Clue," "Breathe," and "Monkey Mind."

4. Draw a picture of a tornado, with all the words that make you worry inside and around it.

Inertia

Riding along in the car of your dreams
Easily coasting—sailing, it seems
Nearing the end, it still holds to its pace
Slow and steady it wins its own race
Weeee—wooo, weeee—wooo, now here we go!
Physics is buckled up safely in tow
An object in motion will remain that way
As Newton's first law still reminds us today
Expand on the rule and sneak right on in
As science is always a good place to begin
To encourage a mood of consistent cheer
Start with a smile—let it go ear to ear
Move onto a laugh, then to a deep roar
And you'll find that your heart will continue to soar
Keep using physics to tame that commotion
While you master the inertia of kinetic emotion.

P.S. I am a science geek at heart. I wrote this poem when I was considering how to apply science to emotion.

We have all experienced inertia at one point or another. Inertia, very simply, is what makes an object that is in motion stay in motion until something of equal force stops it. The opposite is also true: an object that is at rest will stay at rest, unless an equal force is introduced that makes it move again.

This may seem complicated, but it really isn't. Think about riding in a car. You are in the back seat with your own personal chauffeur. All three of you are in motion—you, the car, and your chauffeur. Now, remember the last time you took your seatbelt off before you were supposed to, and the driver hit the brakes unexpectedly? You went flying forward, right? That happened because of inertia. The car stopped moving, but you kept going! The only thing that stopped you from moving was the front seat, which you probably bounced off of. Inertia again! You were in motion, and the only thing that stopped you was something of equal or greater force: the front seat.

There are two lessons that can be learned from this. The first is to keep your seatbelt on! The second is to apply what you've learned to your emotions. Once you know how to get yourself in a good mood, there isn't much that can stop your momentum!

Inertia—I just love the word. I could say it over and over and over again—until someone or something of equal or greater force compelled me to stop.

P.S.S. Questions and Activities for You (and Your Parents Too)

1. If the "inertia" of emotion can affect you for better or worse, do you think your mood can affect others?

2. How have the moods of your family or friends influenced you?

3. What do you think you can do to create a more peaceful atmosphere for yourself and others?

4. Draw an example of a fun way inertia works in real life!

GROW WITH ME POETRY

Draw an example of a fun way inertia works in real life!

Religion

The belief I hold dear, some cannot conceive
But I'm not really bothered if you don't believe
Though to rely only on what your naked eye sees
Is to miss out on the forest because of the trees
A spectrum of faiths like an arching rainbow
Each color a jewel from on high set aglow
Which hue of religion holds God's mighty Seal?
It might be best left to the great cosmic wheel
A spinner to decide which tradition is best
Will only reveal that each one has been blessed
The true intent, that which the arrow has shown
It is never the one that it points to alone
In my humble opinion (I'll share it with care)
But I'll say this with courage and feeling aware
The Light of the world is not cast on one creed
Rather shines from us all with our every good deed.

P.S. This poem was written as I was trying to come to terms with my own religious beliefs. It was during this time that I was finding my spiritual voice drowned out by those spouting their own religious beliefs, without understanding that they were using their belief system as a tool to spread hate instead of love, divisiveness instead of unity, and darkness instead of light.

Since I am an unapologetic Christian, I think I am qualified to note that some Christians do not behave in a Christianly fashion. I have never understood why people leave their manners behind when speaking to those who do not share their religious beliefs. If there was an Eleventh Commandment etched by God, it would surely read, "Thou shalt mind your manners when speaking on My behalf." In a world of What Would Jesus Do? I am continually perplexed by people doing exactly what Jesus would never have done, and in his name to boot!

Setting all biblical and theological differences aside, I believe there is merit and a little of God's light in every religion—and in every person, for that matter, whatever their spiritual beliefs may be. That light is bound to shine brighter in the presence of tolerance toward the many religions of the world, and brightest in the presence of deeds that serve the good of others.

P.S.S. Questions and Activities for You (and Your Parents Too)

1. Describe the God you believe in.

2. Draw a picture of the God you believe in.

3. If you don't necessarily believe in God, draw a circle. Within it, blend together the colors that you think represent "life."

GROW WITH ME POETRY

Draw a picture of the God you believe in.

If you don't necessarily believe in God, draw a circle. Within it, blend together the colors that you think represent "life."

To Have and To Hold

'Til death do us part is what you have said
To love and to cherish and to hold as you wed
Proclaiming your love to all as entwined
Separate lives are now left behind
One husband, one wife, together will be
In marriage, a union of peace you will see
Growing as one, not two split apart
Together are guided, and bound by the heart
Each day that follows this one special day
Hand within hand, a pair you will stay
The path that unravels can never be known
But will always be lit by love that is shown
Grow memories like flowers, tend to them with care
Bathing in kindness and becoming aware
Your brand new beginning has finally been cast
The bright day before you is now here at last
After the kisses, the winks, and toasty warm smiles
Are new husband and wife, having walked
    down the aisle.

P.S. This poem was a gift to my nephew on his wedding day. It is a tribute to him and his most lovely bride.

P.S.S. Questions and Activities for You (and Your Parents Too)

1. Ask your parents or grandparents about their wedding. Perhaps you can pull out their old wedding album or pictures together and reminisce. Write down one of their stories!

2. We live in an age when not all parents are married in a conventional way. Ask your parents about how they met, the challenges they may have faced together, and how they overcame these challenges.

3. Draw a picture of one thing that represents your parents' wedding, or something that symbolizes their relationship—for example, the cake, the rings, the place they were married, or even a heart. Use your imagination; it doesn't have to be conventional!

While You Sleep

I hold your hand at night while you sleep
Please, dear sister, please don't weep
Although I died before you woke
My soul passing on before you ever spoke
Know that I watch you from heaven above
With kindness, care, and unending love

I hold your hand at night while you sleep
And wipe the tears from your soft cheek
Together we'll be and sisters we'll stay
I swell with pride as I see you each day
Thoughtful and tender, loving and sweet
A day will come when again we will meet

Then in heaven I'll hold your hand while we sleep
Our souls together, our love to keep.

P.S. I wrote this poem for my friend of thirty years. She lost her sister when they were both very young. This poem was my gift to her on the anniversary of her sister's death.

Death is such a difficult topic. It forces us to come to terms with an ending, and with that comes a range of emotions that can be hard to explain to people who haven't yet experienced grief. Even if you have never lost someone who was close to you, you may have experienced similar feelings when something else in your life came to an end: the final grade in elementary school (sometimes we unknowingly grieve the end of our innocence), the end of a first love (we grieve for our broken hearts), or perhaps the end of a parent's marriage (we grieve what was). Grief is a powerful emotion, and everyone manages it differently. But gaining insight into this strong and scary feeling can make managing it a bit easier when we are forced to face an "ending" in our life, or the loss of someone we love.

P.S.S. Questions and Activities for You (and Your Parents Too)

1. Write about how you have experienced grief (or an ending) in your own life.

2. What is your favorite memory of what or who you were grieving for?

3. Describe some ways in which people might grieve differently. This might be related to how people show their grief, or even for how long they might process grief internally.

4. Draw a timeline in any shape. Along your timeline, create stops representing the stages of grief. Make the stops into a shape of your choice and color them in with what you think represents the color of grief at that particular point on your line. After you've finished, note how you perceive what a timeline of grief looks like. You might want to show this picture to your parents to see what their thoughts are. Does it reflect their timeline of grief, and how they may have felt during a similar period? If it doesn't, ask them why not.

The Family Tree

What becomes of a family tree
When lightning begets a blackened split?
No longer where it's meant to be
One branch has been directly hit

Yet, was its precious fruit still sound
Though covered in mud, lying bruised and battered?
Yearning to be seen upon the ground
Amongst what the fierce storm winds had scattered

Seeking what once had been held so dear
A kind heart uncovered what the tree once bore,
The fruit was gathered along with the fear
Though buried right down to the earth's deep core

Now the branch kindles a smoldering fire
With the fruit glowing as it ripens under its care
From whence its warmth dries the remnants of ire
And its soft light erases all trace of despair

And thanks to those deep burly roots
That tree's ancestry did survive
Although one limb burned into soot
Its fruit forever sweet did thrive

Such is the life of a great tree
When weathering the storms of its family.

P.S. I hope this poem finds itself dear to the hearts of anyone who has had to weather the storm of a divorce. I wrote this after rereading "To Have and to Hold," thinking how that poem might bring sadness to someone who has suffered through the end of their parents' marriage. I wanted to express that families can still be families even when one "branch" falls from the family tree; and more importantly, that there is always someone to turn to if you need comfort.

Lastly, in those moments when it may feel as if you are that fruit left alone in the rain, this is the time to call on some of the mindfulness skills you have learned. In the midst of the storm, when you're feeling overwhelmed, angry, or sad, call on your breath and listen to yourself breathe. Count your breaths slowly, and when you have settled, call on that special someone. They are there to warm your heart and comfort your soul.

P.S.S. Questions and Activities for You (and Your Parents Too)

1. Write about your experience managing your parents' separation or divorce, or that of a friend's family turmoil.

2. Find, reread, and write down the title of at least one poem from this book that you can revisit to help you when you feel overwhelmed.

3. Draw your Family Tree as you envision it.

Faith

Wrought with worry
Thoughts in a hurry
Spiraling 'round
Frantically abound
Then one little voice
A valuable choice
Innocently spoken
A priceless token
Have faith he did say
In the quietest way
In the wisdom of God
Words to applaud
Blessedly heard
Prophetically stirred
Peace and love
From heaven above.

P.S. I was stunned and left speechless upon hearing the words "Have faith in the wisdom of God," uttered by my then-seven-year-old son. He was about to have an important medical test, a brain scan, that would tell us whether the brain tumor he'd had removed the previous year had grown back. I was fraught with worry and trying not to show a hint of my fear. As he lay down on the table, ready to be slid into the wide mouth of the magnetic resonance machine, he spoke those prophetic words. We would later learn that his tumor had not grown back; and to this day, it never has. Out of the mouths of babes...

P.S.S. Questions and Activities for You (and Your Parents Too)

1. What do you consider to be a miracle? Can there be little, tiny miracles?

2. Think about a time when you experienced an uncanny coincidence. Write how it happened, and the circumstances surrounding it. Do you think it could have been a miracle?

3. Who do you think can guide or inspire a miracle?

4. Draw a picture of something you believe represents faith, peace, or love.

My Angel

One night my heart knocked upon my chest
As if to announce an unforeseen guest
With great trepidation, I lay in my bed
Fully aware, wondering what lay ahead
Then filled with pure love, I soon was embraced
A warmth spreading through me as if I'd been graced
By kaleidoscope colors cast over my eyes
Each ebbing and flowing like the sea's tides
Its waves tumbled slowly, unveiling each hue
Of indigo, orange, and shimmering blue
Feather'd wings all aglow, as if lit from behind
My soul, beams of light, now fully entwined
In wonderful radiance, alluringly bright
A magnificent angel came to visit that night
Now aware of the tears as my eyes started brimming
The heavenly glow before me was dimming
Omnipotence echoing rang in my ears
Then deafening silence as a void reappeared
Tears came even though there was no need to weep
For a seed had been planted, with care and quite deep
This now and always I pray I remember
As I hold on tight to my angel's sweet ember.

P.S. So many of us are smitten with angels. I am in love with this particular angel, because he chose to grace me with his presence one inconsequential night—me, Bridgette Fowler, just a Jane Doe. His presence inspired one poem, then another, and then many—and then Grow with Me Poetry. I take you back to the words "Have faith in the wisdom of God," and remind you that there are no coincidences in life....

P.S.S. Questions and Activities for You (and Your Parents Too)

Fun Fact: While angels are widely cited in biblical or religious contexts, religions all over the world feature stories of benevolent messengers sent to watch over and bring comfort to our earthbound souls. Their presence may be felt at any time, by anyone—believers and nonbelievers alike.

1. What do you think an angel is?

2. What is meant by "an angel on Earth?"

3. What would you do if you met an angel?

4. Draw a picture of what you believe an angel looks like.

The Ripple

A ripple in time

Are the thoughts in our minds

As grains of sand

Gently slip through your hand

A muddle of letters

Strung loosely together

Absorbing emotion

To incite locomotion

Imagine a stone tossed into a pond

A bullseye, the wake to be set forth beyond

Meandering wrinkles

Settling crinkles

A peaceful place

Returning to grace

So too follow your musings

Whispers ensuing

Stillness of mind

A ripple in time.

P.S. A fitting end. I hope this poem brought you back to the act of mindfulness. See your thoughts ease their way in and out, just as ripples in water return to stillness. As a gentle reminder, remove any judgement you may want to insert about your thoughts, and simply love yourself with the full understanding that we are all works in progress, sometimes causing ripples but always able return to a beautifully clean slate.

P.S.S. Questions and Activities for You (and Your Parents Too)

1. Mindfully write your own poem and love it.

2. Mindfully draw your own picture and love it.

Mindfully write your own poem and love it!

Epilogue

P.S. Do you think your poetry experience has come to an end? I'm not so sure! Now that you have made it through this book from front to back, feel free to go back to the beginning and read through the poems again. Maybe you have some favorites. Mark them somehow so that you can go back and reread, update your thoughts, or draw new pictures. Feel free to add your own pages. Take some time to reminisce, look back on how your childhood memories have shaped or are still shaping who you are now, and give yourself some credit for how much you have grown. Once you decide to close the book, tuck it safely away; and then reopen it when you would like to share your experience or re-create it with a special someone.

P.S.S. Do you have a muse? A muse is a person or a personified force that inspires an artist's creativity. My muse was an angel, the very same angel that inspired the poem "My Angel." The more I wrote, the more I found poetry to be a pulpit—one that I could use to share what is dear to me as well as what I felt guided to write about. I'm sure you noticed Grow with Me Poetry's common thread: be kind, you matter; what you say and do matters; and finally, smiling matters.

I was graced with love, light, peace, and words enough to fill this book. From my heart to yours, I invite and encourage you to incorporate these words and the mindful awareness you have mastered with Grow with Me Poetry into each breath that you take, from the moment you wake until the second you sleep.

About the Author

Bridgette Fowler worked in the field of healthcare for thirty years. She began her career in audiology helping the youngest ears hear, and ended it making sure elderly ears could continue to hear the words of their younger counterparts. Today, she is reaching out to all those same ears through her poetry. Writing poems that are both poignant and whimsical, her words speak directly to the issues faced by our youth. She is an avid proponent of mindfulness meditation and touts the practice as a means to keep both mind and body healthy. Additionally, seeing an ever more present disconnect between adults and children, she seeks to bring the generations together by melding her two loves: poetry and mindfulness.

CPSIA information can be obtained
at www.ICGtesting.com
Printed in the USA
BVHW031407240321
603057BV00004B/21